I0666449

CHANNING *of* TANTA

Books in the series
The Buraan Quartet
by E. M. Clifford

Galloway of Buraan
Graybill of Azianlu
Prior of Kazachi Post
Channing of Tanta

CHANNING *of* TANTA

E. M. CLIFFORD

RESOURCE *Publications* · Eugene, Oregon

CHANNING OF TANTA

Copyright © 2025 E. M. Clifford. All rights reserved. Except for brief quotations in critical publications or reviews, no part of this book may be reproduced in any manner without prior written permission from the publisher. Write: Permissions, Wipf and Stock Publishers, 199 W. 8th Ave., Suite 3, Eugene, OR 97401.

Resource Publications
An Imprint of Wipf and Stock Publishers
199 W. 8th Ave., Suite 3
Eugene, OR 97401

www.wipfandstock.com

PAPERBACK ISBN: 979-8-3852-3198-0
HARDCOVER ISBN: 979-8-3852-3199-7
EBOOK ISBN: 979-8-3852-3200-0
VERSION NUMBER 01/09/25

Cover Images: Member of the Class of 1921. Class Photos Collection, William Smith Morton Library Archives, Union Presbyterian Seminary. Used by permission.

Map of Tanta (detail). Egypt Town Series. Surveyed 1924–26, published 1928 by Maslahat al-Misahah. American Geographical Society Library Digital Map Collection, University of Wisconsin, Milwaukee.

Portrait of a Man (Bir Bey Portresi). Ottoman Imperial Archives, ca. 1910.

*For a young man who knows kindness and integrity
as his closest friends*

Jesus said, Thou shalt love the LORD thy God

With all thy heart, with all thy soul, and with all thy mind

This is the first and great commandment

And the second is like unto it

Thou shalt love thy neighbor as thyself

On these two commandments hang all of the Law and the Prophets

MATTHEW 22:37–40

PREFACE

U NLIKE the other locations I have written about in the past, Egypt is
well known to people in my likely readership. Nearly every ten-year-
old child goes through a school unit on the treasures of Egypt's Pharaonic
civilization. Is there a person anywhere who does not recognize a photo
of the Pyramids?

The time period in which this story unfolds, however, is far less familiar, probably all but unknown outside the tourism sector and the history
of Egyptology. Yet it is a crucial turning point in Egypt's development as
a modern nation. From 1910 to 1930, Egypt broke out against centuries
of foreign domination, achieving an indigenous rebellion against Ottoman and British imperialism. It began to resist the cultural hegemony of
the West. It struggled against the heavy hand of England's economic and
military power. It moved from a static and mostly medieval structure of
traditional religion to a radically new concept of powerful political Islam. It
began to face the need for social justice for the poor, and the full humanity
of women. And it grappled with the decidedly mixed legacy of Western
Christian missionary work in Egypt since the early nineteenth century.

All of the events in this narrative are based upon actual incidents, such
as the infamous Denshawai conflict, and the crisis surrounding Turkiya
Hasan. But the timeline of the events of this era has been somewhat com-
pressed in the telling. The Denshawai conflict took place in 1906, while the
"Orphan Scandal" involving Turkiya (which inspired Benjamin Channing's
fateful mishap) happened in 1933. The official founding of the Muslim
Brotherhood by Hasan al-Banna occurred in 1928, as did the notorious
Samuel Zwemer confrontation at al-Azhar. And Channing's illness has
connections with the abortive mission of William Whiting Borden and his
death in Cairo in 1913 (see *Borden of Yale*).

Apart from the timeline, I have made other small modifications and adjustments, intended to aid in comprehension and deliver important information. Please note that I have not followed any technical scheme in the transliteration of Arabic, but reproduced the sounds of the language in a way that I hope will work for English speakers.

Likewise—as in all of my books—the condescending, bigoted, hostile, essentializing language expressed by certain characters is taken nearly verbatim from the sources.

The wealth of pertinent primary and scholarly sources for the study of this era is extraordinary. In the "Selected Sources," I have refrained from listing many useful earlier books that set the stage for what was to come, such as Andrew Watson's *The American Mission in Egypt* and Charles Watson's *Egypt and the Christian Crusade*. I have reluctantly omitted some entertaining but less relevant sources, such as the Amelia B. Edwards classic *A Thousand Miles up the Nile* (1877, 1888). I have not included highly influential works of interpretation that concentrate on neighboring areas—studies by Abdul Latif Tibawi or Albert Hourani, for example. Instead, I have placed emphasis upon the more specialized and obscure sources that are so rewarding for the researcher to find, and that may be especially interesting to readers.

Presbyterians are famous for their tradition of doing everything "decently and in order." That certainly applies to mission boards, agencies, associations, and committees, when it comes to keeping records, minutes, financial accounts, and annual reports. A trove of detailed contemporary evidence (though with clear biases or points of view) is provided in the voice of those who were deeply engaged in the work.

Access to these and other valuable materials was made possible by the wonderful staff of the William Smith Morton Library at Union Presbyterian Seminary (especially the Reference Librarian, Dr. Mengistu Lemma), and the courteous professionals at the Presbyterian Historical Society in Philadelphia. Many thanks to you all.

I also draw upon the personal experiences of ten years living and working in Egypt. That is barely enough time to scratch the surface of Egypt's richness, to touch lightly upon its history, to absorb a little of its manifold cultures. I offer this book as a small gift to the many Egyptians whom I love and admire—Muslim, Orthodox, Catholic, and Protestant. And I salute the many expatriates who have done their best to make a contribution to Egypt's society.

Rabbina ma'akum.

May our Lord be with you.

OCTOBER 1922–NOVEMBER 1923

CHAPTER 1

WHEN they were told that the ambulance had arrived from Port Said, both doctors went downstairs at once to meet it.

Dr. Hessburgh got down there first, since he had just finished with another patient. His junior colleague, Dr. Mourad Wahba, met him only a moment later. They saw the ambulance attendant and a hospital orderly unloading a field stretcher with a covered figure on it, a person who should have been lying still but was thrashing about in a way that made the stretcher difficult to carry.

A dazed-looking young man climbed down from the ambulance cab with his arms full of the patient's jacket and other belongings. This young man followed the stretcher wherever it went, evidently obeying someone's orders.

"This way, to the stairs," said Philip Hessburgh. "Do you need another hand with that?"

The bearers refused any help and took their awkward burden up to the hospital's third floor and into one of the two private suites reserved for those willing and able to pay for them.

Waiting in the room were the two American nurses, Miss Tate and Miss McCaul. With the bearers holding the stretcher close, the four of them slipped their hands under the patient and deftly shifted him to the bed. This amount of motion set off a spasm of coughing, followed by groans of distress.

The stretcher-bearers tried to leave, and that is when they realized the young man who had been following them was still there, standing in the doorway.

"These are his things," said the young man. "May I leave them with you? I'm not really supposed to be here."

"No, don't leave yet," said Doctor Mourad. "We need to know how long the patient has been like this."

"Only a few days, I think. That is, he was ill for about a week—the Spanish flu, someone said. Couldn't come to worship on Sunday. But then he must have got better, because he was able to lead the Wednesday evening Bible study. Then I didn't see him for a couple of days, though I didn't think anything of it, because we were all busy packing up our things and getting ready to disembark at Port Said. He's not one to mope around and complain. So I wasn't aware that he was so sick until we were about to tie up at the dock and he just fell to pieces."

"Influenza first? Then he got a bit better, and now this?"

"I think so. It all happened so fast there at the dock. The consul sent people to meet us because there were several Americans on board. And when we found poor Channing like this, they immediately got an ambulance from the Canal Company and bundled him into it, and they told me to get in too and make sure he got to Tanta Hospital. So that's why I'm here. But all of my things have been sent on to Cairo and I'm supposed to report *there*, not to Tanta, so I need to find a way to get myself there as soon as I can."

"There is an evening train, about 8:15. Ask downstairs at reception."

"That won't be necessary," came a voice from behind the young man. "Mrs. Zwemer and I are here from Cairo with the motorcar, so you can go into the city with us. If you are willing to stay in Tanta until we are sure Mr. Channing will be all right."

At this Doctor Hessburgh looked up from the patient's bedside. "If all of you would kindly remove yourselves to the sitting room, we have a patient to care for."

As the excess persons were ushered out, Doctor Mourad caught a glimpse of a whole collection of people in the outer room, apparently all of them American missionaries, conversing in anxious tones.

The two special suites on the third floor served the needs of prominent persons in town, and were equipped with a bedroom, a private bath, and a sizable sitting room where the inevitable squadron of relatives could come and gather. The door between these rooms could be closed and that is exactly what happened next.

They began to undress the patient carefully, trying to jostle him as little as possible. The ambulance attendant had loosened his tie, but they had to remove that along with his fine linen shirt, deeply stained with sweat. It was obvious that the patient had a high fever without needing to use a thermometer. They pulled off his shoes, excellent leather Oxfords marked inside with a label reading *MacKendrick's of Boston*. His tweed trousers matched the jacket the young man had thrust upon them. He wore underclothes of top quality as well. Soon they had the poor soul as naked as a baby upon the hospital bed.

Tall and broad-shouldered, an athletic build. Early twenties. Clearly very fit, before this infection took hold of him. But now, he was struggling to take in air, nostrils flaring, very frequent, labored, shallow breathing. His cheeks were flushed, eyes unfocused, and an eruption of small blisters encircled his bluish lips.

His pulse was strong and there were good heart sounds, to which both doctors listened at length. Philip Hessburgh tapped the patient's chest with his fingertips in several places and lingered over the lower left side of his ribcage.

"I'd like to start him on a half-grain of codeia, to ease the pain and coughing. Do you agree?"

"I do," replied Doctor Mourad. "I advise against any other interventions until we know the distinct type of organism in that lung. I'd like to slip out and prepare an Avery culture medium."

"That's just what I'd like you to do, so thank you."

Doctor Mourad moved to leave the room, then said, "I thought that this patient only just arrived in Egypt. How is it that he has accumulated such an entourage?"

"Reverend Zwemer is the acting chief administrator of the American Mission in Egypt, in the absence of Reverend Alexander. He is responsible for all of us. There is a great deal of interest in this young man, in particular. His arrival has been eagerly awaited. If we can't save *this* patient . . . there could be consequences."

Mourad glanced at him doubtfully. "I'm sorry . . . I don't understand."

Doctor Hessburgh looked tired, and troubled. He waved one hand vaguely. "It's too much to explain just now. I'll go into it fully later. Apart from all that . . . you will be the attending physician on this case. You are our pulmonary specialist and this is very obviously lung disease. You will need to report all developments to Mr. Zwemer as you would to next of kin. Is that all right?"

"Yes, of course, Doctor."

When Mourad opened the door to the sitting room, he was quickly surrounded by American missionaries pressing him for information about the patient. "Mr. Zwemer, this young man is quite ill, evidently with acute lobar pneumonia. I believe he is suffering from a bacterial infection following a viral illness. I intend to culture the organism and then I shall be able to select the specific treatment."

"Where is Doctor Hessburgh?" someone demanded.

Mourad ignored this. "If you will excuse me, time is of the essence." He began working his way toward the door.

Behind him, a woman's voice said distinctly, "You know, at the C.M.S. clinic they lost their English doctor, and they tried to replace him with a young Egyptian Christian man. But the Egyptians have no confidence in their own people, in spite of all this outcry about self-rule, so attendance at the dispensary fell away at once."

Mourad ignored this, too.

In the hospital laboratory, he prepared a sterile sample container, coating it with agar mixed with beef broth. By the time he returned to the patient's room, Doctor Hessburgh had departed, and one of the two nurses, Miss McCaul, was there at bedside. She had provided the patient with a pillow and covered him with a clean sheet and a warm blanket. The injection of codeine had quieted his struggling.

Mourad was a stellar graduate of Asyut College and a former resident in pulmonary medicine at the Qasr al-Aini military hospital. He knew pneumonia when he saw it. He also knew the frighteningly high case-fatality rate of bacterial infection following influenza, especially in younger men, aged 20–40, who were otherwise healthy.

Pneumonia was sometimes called "the old man's friend," because it could terminate the death struggle of the elderly in a merciful way. But its power to carry off the young was clearly documented in the fierce outbreak of influenza in 1918 and 1919, which was still very much in circulation, especially in the autumn and winter. The initial viral disease could weaken pulmonary resistance, leaving the lungs vulnerable to secondary infection by common bacterial pathogens in the general population. In close settings such as hospital wards, military barracks, mines, and ships at sea, exposure was almost unavoidable.

The patient opened his eyes when Mourad leaned over him with a stethoscope. His face was pinched together, extremely pale, with hectic red blotches on his cheeks. He was trembling with the chills that often accompanied a high fever.

He did have some mental clarity, however, enough to recognize Mourad as one of his doctors. "What . . ." Channing croaked, "is . . . it?"

"Please don't try to speak. It will only increase the coughing and the pain. I can tell you that you have an infection with serious lung involvement. I'm going to examine a sputum sample to determine which microorganism is responsible. Then we should be able to select the appropriate treatment. Do you understand?"

Squinting through his pain, Ben Channing nodded.

"All right, then. I have a sterile sample receptacle here," said Mourad, showing him the glass petri dish lined with agar. "When I take off the lid, I want you to bring up some sputum from deep in the lungs, a very deep cough, even though I fear it will hurt you. If you just try to take a full breath it will likely follow. Then you should expectorate into the dish." Channing nodded again.

He tried to open his lungs for a full breath and triggered a massive spasm of coughing, which spewed thick rust-colored secretions not only into the dish, but all over the doctor's hands and face and clothing.

Gasping, he sank back on the pillow. "Sorry!" he mouthed silently. "Sorry! Sorry!"

"Never mind," said the doctor calmly. "*Maalish.* Doesn't matter. I'll get this sample processed as soon as the organism has grown in the culture medium. I'll take it to the laboratory now."

Doctor Mourad tried to straighten up to leave the bedside, but Ben suddenly grasped his upper arm tightly. Mourad was surprised by the patient's muscular strength. "What's wrong?" asked Mourad. "Do you need something?"

Channing's eyes were full of pain, but he managed to mouth some words. "Pray . . . for me."

Mourad was taken aback by this. He replied, "But I am a Muslim."

Channing gripped him with desperate firmness and mouthed again very slowly, "Pray . . . for . . . me."

Mourad stood still for a moment, then moved aside the bedcovers, and stroked with his hand the left side of Channing's bare chest. "*Allahumma,*" he recited, "*Rabb an-naas . . .*" Completing the traditional prayer for the sick, he then repeated it in English. "O Allah, Lord of the people! Remove the harm and heal him. For You are the Healer, and there is no healing but Yours, with a healing that leaves no illness behind."

Channing released his grip and his hand dropped weakly beside him. Mourad covered his patient with the sheet and blanket. Channing mouthed silently to him, "Thank you." The doctor motioned to Miss McCaul to take his place at the bedside, then carried his glass sample dish out of the room.

Benjamin Channing was taken on a gurney to the x-ray room for an image of his chest. The x-ray machine was an old gas-tube model: loud, smelly, and slow, with a real danger of injury by burning. Mourad had to operate the machine himself, since most of the staff were afraid to go near it. He hesitated to use it in most cases. But he really wanted to have a look at the suspected mass in Channing's left lung.

And there it was, thick and threatening, an alien growth inside Channing's body.

After several hours of development, the culture did reveal a fixed type of diplococcus, Type I. That was good in a way, because Mourad knew that he could send for a specific horse serum for Type I from the Qasr al-Aini hospital in Cairo. This he did at once. But Mourad also knew that in every one hundred cases of lobar pneumonia, thirty-five were due to Type I infection—and of these, ten patients died. He also knew that serological treatment could be effective in Type I, but also had numerous serious risks of its own.

Armed with this diagnostic information, he headed for the sitting room where Channing's entourage was waiting.

"Mr. Zwemer," he began. "I have a clear idea now what is causing Mr. Channing's illness. He has a Type I pneumonia that is well advanced. We can combat it with serum treatments that have shown some success. Untreated cases of this type have a mortality rate of about thirty percent. With a high-titre serum, that rate has been reduced to seven or eight percent."

"Mortality rate!" exclaimed a hard thin woman, all angles and edges. "Does Doctor Hessburgh agree with your diagnosis?"

"Miss Bostram, please," said Mr. Zwemer. "I am sure that Doctor—Mourad, is it?—is well acquainted with these cases."

"I think I know how he got this," interjected the young man who had come there with Channing in the ambulance. "I heard that there was illness among the ship's crew. Ben was always going down into the crew quarters to visit with them. He spoke some Spanish, you see, and he wanted to be friendly with them down there."

"Spanish?" asked Doctor Mourad.

"Yes, the crew was mostly Puerto Rican. He went down to chat with them and do some Bible meetings for them. He was very popular with the sailors, certainly."

"So, little wonder he's ill," Miss Bostram sniffed.

"I'll begin treatment as soon as the serum arrives from Cairo. I want you to know that the treatment itself is not without possible complications. Mr. Channing is still in danger and may be so for ten to fourteen days. You should consider this when making your own plans."

"Yes, thank you, Doctor. We shall organize a bedside vigil to ensure that some of us are present here at all times." Mourad became aware of a tiny woman sitting close beside Samuel Zwemer, with a weary pleading face, who never stopped nodding and smiling slightly. He recognized the behavior of an intimidated woman. Zwemer himself seemed to have only one facial expression, a severe and dignified frown, with deep creases beside his nose and mouth.

Doctor Hessburgh came upstairs presently with the horse serum that had just been delivered from Cairo. Horses were deliberately infected with fixed-type pathogens, and once they produced plenty of antibodies, their blood was drawn and an amber-colored, protein-rich liquid was separated from it. This antibody boost could enable a patient to fight off the infectious agent in his own bloodstream . . . but it also introduced many other foreign elements which, if the patient reacted badly to them, could kill him.

Philip Hessburgh and Mourad Wahba planned to try a series of sensitization tests first, before giving their patient a therapeutic dose.

Mourad prepared two syringes. One of them contained a tiny amount of horse serum diluted with nine parts of sterile saline. The other syringe contained saline solution only. Mourad injected the test solution into Channing's left arm, while Hessburgh injected the control solution into his right. Almost immediately, a raised welt appeared at the site of the serum injection, and soon became as thick and firm as a coat button. Soon after this, the skin around the welt was flooded with subcutaneous blood, like a very purple bruise.

They waited one hour, watching Channing carefully.

As no further reaction occurred, they prepared the next test. Mourad measured one cubic centimeter of serum, diluted with an equal amount of sterile saline. Then he used a little flame warmer to bring it close to body temperature. As Hessburgh stood by with a syringe of adrenaline, Mourad slowly injected the serum into the patient's median cubital vein.

They both stood over him, looking for signs of anaphylaxis. Twenty minutes, thirty minutes, an hour passed, and there was no systemic crisis. Both doctors began to breathe a bit easier.

The next test involved fifteen cubic centimeters—about three teaspoons—of serum solution, in a syringe with a rubber tube, easing the liquid gradually by means of gravity into the patient's vein. Channing's skin flushed red and perspiration increased.

"Thermal reaction," said Mourad to Hessburgh. He nodded.

At last they felt it was safe to administer the therapeutic dose, one hundred cubic centimeters of serum, warmed and placed into a small intravenous drip. It took twenty minutes for the liquid to pass into Channing's vein, as both doctors stood attentively beside him.

This time, Ben's temperature suddenly rose, and there was profuse sweating, then chills. Poor Ben was mostly unaware of all of this drama, as he floated in a codeine haze keeping him quiet and still. They watched him constantly but did not reach for the syringe of adrenaline; a thermal reaction was typical and not a sign of allergic anaphylaxis.

"Doctor Hessburgh, if you need to go, I will do bedside. I may need you again in four to eight hours."

"Thank you, Mourad," said the older man. "With your permission, I think I'll go out and brief Zwemer and the others on what we've done so far."

Mourad smiled a little. "That would be very kind of you," he said.

The antibody treatment did not kill their patient. In fact, he began to make steady and gratifying progress.

The coughing became less violent and painful, and Channing lost his pinched and squinting look. His eyes widened to an innocent openness that puzzled Mourad until he realized that this was Ben's normal expression.

When it seemed that the patient was out of mortal danger, the Zwemers returned to Cairo, leaving the resident Tanta mission staff to occupy the patient's sitting room and receive all updates. Unfortunately that included Joan Bostram, of the Mary Clokey Porter Boarding School for Girls, but also Rev. and Mrs. Peter Reed, a friendly and gentle young couple of Mourad's age, about thirty. Peter Reed was pastor-evangelist for the Gharbiya district, while Lydia Reed cared for their two children, ages six and three.

When one or both of the Reeds were present, Mourad's briefings were easy. Miss Bostram, however, seemed to resent the patient's improvement, since it gave her less to blame Mourad for.

Seven days into the treatment, Channing abruptly broke out in fierce bumpy red wheals and itchy blotches. They had to bind his hands in gauze mittens to stop him scratching at the maddening rash.

Examining him, Mourad saw swelling of the joints, especially the ankles and elbows. Moving his limbs caused Channing to suck in his breath with pain.

Mourad asked Doctor Hessburgh to have a look. "What do you think?"

"It's serum sickness, isn't it?"

"I believe so . . . the animal proteins in the serum cause a histamine reaction. He will be miserable for several days. I've stopped the serum treatments . . . he'll have to continue to combat the pneumonia on his own. Adrenaline may reduce the symptoms, and I'll ask Miss McCaul to begin oatmeal baths."

"You know what you're doing, Mourad. You don't need me to confirm."

"A second opinion, then," said the younger man. "By the way, I do think it's time you explained to me the facts about our premium patient. People here behave as though he were the Prince of Wales."

Doctor Hessburgh sighed a bit. "Everyone in the United States has heard of the Channings. They're like the Rockefeller family. Ben's grandfather Ezra Channing developed the air brake for railway cars. We learn about it in school, like Eli Whitney and the cotton gin."

"Giants of the industrial revolution. I think I remember that from Asyut College."

"Well, these are the same Channings. Immense personal fortune. Ben's father died suddenly a few years ago—it was in all the papers—and his older brother James took over the business, which now has a major Wall Street component. It seems all they have to do now is sit back and let their money make more money."

"So, young Benjamin is free to go out and find himself on the mission field."

"That's about it. Of course, it's very much a feather in our cap to attract such a promising young man to the American Mission. Zwemer and Mott and Speer and the others, they're constantly writing and giving speeches about the caliber of candidates who need to come forward for the Lord's work in remote places, where they can be heroes for the Gospel, and so forth. And now among us is the candidate of their dreams. It would be a trifle awkward if he came out here and immediately expired."

"I see what you mean."

"Now we need to see if we can somehow prevent his turning into another Samuel Zwemer." The two of them shared a glance of complete mutual understanding.

When the serum sickness abated, Channing felt so much better that they began to allow him to be up and out of bed. They found him some striped cotton pajamas and a cozy bathrobe. He started spending time on the balcony outside his room, in the warm October sunshine. Still weak and very short of breath, he could not manage much more than that.

From this third-floor vantage point, he could see the outer edges of the town of Tanta spread out before him, forming a large triangle between the two urban canals. To the east, beyond the Quhafa Canal, lay the American Mission girls' boarding school, the domain of Miss Bostram and her colleagues. A large area of open earth lay a bit beyond it, still American Mission property.

Immediately to the north of the hospital—right below his rooms, really—there was a large developed complex of buildings that he did not recognize at first. He began watching them at various times of day to see what took place there.

To the west, beside the inner edge of the al-Qasid Canal, was evidently a secondary school for boys. The noise emanating from this complex at all hours of the school day was the primary clue. But he could also see crowds of teenagers flowing in and out and spending a good deal of time in a large open football ground, running around randomly, organizing games, pushing and shoving, doing high-energy adolescent boy things.

To the other side of the football ground lay another school-like complex, but built in a quadrangle shape, with a courtyard in the center. A high wall with wire along the top enclosed the facility. It seemed odd to have two large schools almost adjoining but sharing no space between them.

Channing saw somewhat older boys in the secure complex, and none of the rough but playful behavior he had witnessed at the other school. These boys, when outdoors, sat on benches, walked around and around the courtyard in groups, or did supervised calisthenics lined up in rows. Most of their day was spent in a sullen silence.

One afternoon as he was looking down at them, Ben saw a scuffle break out at the walled school. This was not the kind of horseplay that took place at the other school, but a serious wrestling match and fistfight. A circle of boys quickly formed to watch. They jostled for position and began to yell support for one fighter or the other.

Then Ben saw several uniformed men moving to break up the fight, carrying short heavy sticks. They used these truncheons to prod the on-lookers away from the scene, sometimes dealing a smart blow to one's shoulders or legs.

This violence was done in a routine, methodical way, without excitement. Ben Channing looked on with alarm.

The two fighting boys were pulled apart and beaten, until they submitted to the tying of their wrists behind them. Then they were marched away toward one of the buildings.

Ben thought about what he had seen until the next time Mourad came to check on him.

"Doctor," he began, "Can you tell me what buildings those are, below the hospital?"

"Well, on the left there is the boys' government school. Secondary level. And on the right is the youth reformatory."

"I see . . . that explains a few things."

"You're looking a bit brighter today, Mr. Channing. Let me listen to your lungs and heart." Mourad placed his stethoscope on Channing's back. "Can you take a deeper breath?"

"I can, but it does hurt, and it makes me cough."

"Yes, I'm sorry." There were signs of improvement, but his patient had a ways to go yet.

Ben began to sneak out of his room and walk the halls of the hospital. At first he had to stop frequently and sit down, but soon he could move around the building fairly well, and even—slowly—up and down the stairs. The Tanta hospital was rebuilt during the Great War and the new facility was clean and welcoming. It was by far the best medical care provider in Lower Egypt, between Cairo and the Mediterranean Sea. Clinics dependent upon it had been established in several Delta villages.

He learned that it had actually been founded as a women's hospital in the 1890s, by two female American doctors, Anna B. Watson and Caroline Lawrence. By 1915, more than one third of the doctors serving in the American Mission were women, even though women made up less than three percent of the new graduates from American medical schools. There was latitude for them to serve abroad that seldom existed in hospital or private practice at home.

But now the new building had room for both male and female patients, in separate wards. There was also an active hospital ministry, led by a kindly Egyptian Protestant pastor, Rev. Gayyid, an evangelist named Boulos, and a remarkable elderly blind Bible Woman known widely as Sitt Shemsa, who shared her apparently inexhaustible supply of memorized Bible verses with everyone.

Each morning before the outpatient clinic opened, there was a half-hour worship service in the waiting area and garden, with singing, prayer and a brief encouraging message. No one was compelled to attend, but since they were already there waiting, it required more effort to avoid it.

Channing at first felt self-conscious about going to worship in his housecoat and pajamas, but he soon realized that almost all of the men were wearing long, loose, white or light-blue gowns very much like an old-fashioned nightshirt: not just the patients, but most of the visitors and relatives. The women generally wore big black all-encompassing wraps over their long dresses. The few men wearing Western-style suits and ties with a red fez or *tarboush* on their heads belonged to the *effendi*, the educated clerical or professional class, including the pastors and doctors, and some outpatients seeking care.

Ben observed the chaplaincy staff and their helpers at their work. He listened and learned. They moved slowly and quietly throughout the building, offering a bit of caring and comfort to the suffering, the frightened, the bereaved.

Most of the inpatients were surgical cases, and they were kept in the hospital until their wounds were fully healed, since they rarely had homes to go to that were appropriate places for recovery from an operation. They enjoyed the cleanliness and peace, their dressings were properly changed, and infection was kept to a minimum. But that meant they were often on the wards convalescing after they began to feel better, with very little to do. So the visits of the chaplains were a welcome friendly respite in an uneventful day.

The chaplain's assistants had also been trained in basic nursing support skills, so they helped to bring fresh drinking water to patients, serve them their meals, and keep the wards in order. At the same time, they offered words of God's love, a passage of Scripture, a moment of prayer. It was all the more remarkable, really, since nearly all of their patients were Muslim.

Lower Egypt, where the Nile fanned out into a network of streams and canals feeding the rich farmland on its way to the sea, was ninety-eight percent Muslim. The few Christians lived mainly in or near Alexandria, or were government workers sent there from Cairo or Upper Egypt. The American Mission had always found the Delta to be nearly impervious to Christian influence.

They relied almost entirely on modeling a gentle human empathy: the *ruh al-khidma*, or spirit of service. A fellow-feeling toward sick or injured people as immortal souls valued by God just like themselves . . . the kind of compassion that inspires trust. Doctor Hessburgh and his team had determined that there was no successful medical treatment without this. Impersonal technical intervention was not enough, no matter how expertly applied.

They also made a conscious effort to display harmonious and respectful relationships among the hospital staff. They considered this, too, a form of evangelism. No lying, swearing, insults or harsh words were permitted among them.

Channing happened to be present when one patient spoke angrily to another, accusing him of tampering with his belongings. The evangelist Boulos said mildly to him, "We don't use that kind of language here." That deflected the man's ire onto Boulos, who endured his abuse without comment. When the patient's anger was spent, Boulos helped him to find the missing article he had accused his neighbor of stealing.

The staff members were not perfect, not by any means. But they were firmly committed to their calling. And just as peer pressure can have a corrupting influence, it can also reinforce positive patterns. It was interesting to watch this process unfold.

On the twentieth day of Channing's stay at the American Mission Hospital, Philip Hessburgh came into his room and found the patient standing on his balcony, fully clothed.

"Going somewhere, Mr. Channing?"

"Oh . . . hello, Doctor. Miss Tate was kind enough to get my linen washed and my suit cleaned and pressed. I feel almost like a proper human being, now."

"It's providential in a way, because Doctor Mourad and I want to talk with you about discharge. I wouldn't say you're in perfectly sound shape, but you've made good progress, and I don't think you need to be treated as an inpatient any longer."

"So happy to hear you say that! I mean, I am eternally grateful for everything you've done for me here. But I'm just lounging about now, while life is out *there*, passing me by."

"Did anyone tell you that your trunks arrived from Port Said? The consulate brought them through customs for you. They are in a storeroom downstairs. Holding them for you until you move in somewhere."

"I don't actually know where I'm supposed to go. I believe I need to report to Mr. Zwemer in Cairo, for some kind of orientation. I gather that the new people are housed in an apartment together in the city near the American University, where they take instruction in Arabic and classes about Islam, Egyptian history and so on. I don't want to sound like a know-it-all, but I've already done a lot of that in college. Not much desire to repeat it."

Hessburgh smiled inwardly. This was going better than he expected.

"I'm sure such training is altogether appropriate for most of the beginners," the doctor said. "But I confess, I have my doubts about it. For instance, I don't like the plan of housing the new people together, in Cairo, or upcountry in Asyut. I mean, it's good for group cohesiveness, but people will naturally spend most of their time with each other, speaking English and falling into routines that are already familiar, mostly among Christians. That may not be the best way to learn and adapt."

"I would like to become a part of life in Egypt as soon as possible."

"Of course you would, and the best way to do that is to live and work among the people, don't you think? When I first came out here as a young doctor almost thirty years ago, I was assigned to the village of Danasur here in the Delta, where I was the only missionary and the only English speaker. I had to adapt very quickly, I assure you."

"Really, I believe that's what I want."

"It's not entirely up to you, of course," the doctor continued, "Because the Delta Evangelistic Committee has some responsibility for deciding who will serve where, and in what capacity. But if you stay here in Tanta or in the vicinity, I think I can promise you that kind of cultural immersion." Hessburgh and Channing sat down on the balcony in a couple of wicker armchairs. "And there is another thing. You have studied some Arabic at Yale, have you not? I will disclose that I have seen your résumé."

"Yes . . . I did two years with Professor Henderson and a lot of graduate students, mostly doing classical Arabic."

"Very wise."

"And I must say, I really loved it. It was like the code languages we used to make up when we were boys, a lot of secret writing and such. At the Hampton School we all knew Latin and Greek, so we had to innovate to come up with new alphabets and made-up words. Arabic seems a lot like that."

Hessburgh noted Ben's enthusiasm. "Mr. Zwemer and the head of the Anglican mission in Cairo, Temple Gairdner, have devised a course of study for the new recruits that involves learning colloquial Arabic through the Roman alphabet. That's what they teach now in the American University's School of Oriental Studies. I'll be frank—I find this appalling. Yes, it's quicker and easier for most, and it's probably good enough for many purposes, but no Egyptian will ever respect you for it. They are justly proud of their beautiful language and if you don't learn it properly they will never listen to you. And if these new workers don't learn the written language, they remain functionally illiterate."

"My reading and writing are far from perfect, but I can get by, I think."

"You'll need to do much more than get by. And the courses they are pushing in Cairo will never get you there."

"I understand."

Hessburgh frowned and stood up. "It's possible that I am telling you this because you have a right to know—an honorable motivation. It's also possible that I am saying this because I detest Mr. Zwemer and I don't want you to fall under his spell."

Channing looked up at him in surprise. At that moment, Doctor Mourad entered the room.

Philip Hessburgh said, "Doctor Mourad will be responsible for treating you as an outpatient. I'll leave you to discuss it."

When he had gone, Mourad said, "It looks as if you are ready to leave right now."

"Well, I might be, if I had somewhere to go."

"Yes . . . I wanted to raise that with you. I agree that you are ready for discharge, but I advise you to stay in Tanta for at least two weeks, so that I may monitor the healing of your lungs. You experienced some damage to the left lower lobe and it will take time to clear."

"Do you mean, stay in a hotel or something?"

"I have another suggestion. Some friends of mine share an apartment nearby. They are young unmarried men, appointed to the government school as teachers, from the Dar al-'Ulum in Cairo. They speak some

English but they are far more comfortable in Arabic. It might be a good way for you to work on the spoken language."

"Doctor, that's a wonderful idea!"

"Call me Mourad, please. I'd like to think that we are friends now."

"More than friends, I would say. I don't know exactly how to relate to a person who has saved my life."

"*Alhamdu lillah*," Mourad replied. "Praise to God, the Healer. Thanks and praise."

"Indeed, I'm very thankful." Channing smiled. "Doctor Hessburgh will be happy. He doesn't want me to settle in Cairo and join the basic training for new recruits. He thinks I can learn more in the Delta by living with Egyptians and staying away from the fleshpots and tourist traps of the big city."

"Philip Hessburgh is perhaps the wisest man I know. If that is his counsel, I think you should heed it."

"I would appreciate having a place to stay for the next couple of weeks, anyway. After that, I will need to go to the American Mission headquarters in Cairo to get my paperwork in order. And figure out exactly what will happen next."

"Ben, I'll make a pact with you. At the end of your convalescence, I shall personally take you to Cairo to the Ezbekiya office of the American Mission to work things out with the bosses. And then I'll show you the Pyramids of Giza, just to offer you some perspective on the pettiness of our little concerns in the vast panorama of human history."

"Yes! There is so much that I want to see and do."

"Patience . . . *shweya bi shweya. Khatwa bi khatwa.* Step by step."

When the day of discharge came, Channing went down to the bursar's office to pay his hospital bill. He was told that, as a member of the American Mission in Egypt, he was treated free of charge. He thought for a minute, and then wrote out a personal check on the Bank of New Haven for four thousand dollars.

"It's a donation," he explained. "Buy Doctor Mourad a new x-ray machine."

The bursar was floored by this and took the check to show to Philip Hessburgh, who merely nodded.

They moved his rather extensive luggage into the apartment he was to share on Muhammad Pasha Said Street, just beyond Tanta's municipal garden. It was a spacious old place, on the first floor, with very high ceilings, huge windows, and a long hallway with apparently six or eight bedrooms.

Only one of the other residents was there when he and Mourad arrived, in the middle of the day.

"Abbas! Here is the new lodger I told you about. Benjamin Channing."

Abbas offered his hand. "My name is Abbas Bahri. *Ahlan wa sahlan.*" Welcome.

"*Ahlan beek,*" replied Channing bashfully.

"He speaks Arabic already," Abbas said with a smile. "You said we must teach him to speak, Mourad."

"You happened to choose one of the dozen words I can usually pull out of my hat," Ben replied.

"Hat?" repeated Abbas. It soon became apparent that there would be a slow process of communication between them.

Abbas showed him around the flat. It was very modest, with the simplest furnishings, and did look very much like several unmarried men lived there. But the rooms were large and there was a mattress on an iron bedstead for him to use, a wooden desk, a chair, and a big old painted wardrobe. He would need to buy some things, such as sheets, blankets and towels, and a share of food for the kitchen. Abbas offered to take him to the local shops that afternoon.

First, they went to the Bank Misr, to change some of Channing's dollars into Egyptian pounds and piastres. On a street full of basic housewares, they bought the cottons he would need, a metal pitcher and washbasin, and a colorful *shanta* or cloth tote bag to use to carry his shower kit back and forth to the bathroom.

Closer to home, they stopped at the *baal* or grocer's shop to stock up on the supplies he had to contribute to their kitchen. Abbas was teaching him words and phrases the whole time: rice, potatoes, spinach, onions. Cucumbers, tomatoes, oranges, olive oil. Vocabulary that, for some reason, they had failed to cover in Professor Henderson's Arabic classes at Yale.

All of the walking and carrying of bundles exhausted Ben. He needed to stop and rest several times, while Abbas regarded him with concern. When they had returned to the flat, he urged Ben to lie down and rest until dinner.

When Ben awoke, he could hear several masculine voices in the communal sitting room. He ventured out to find his six new roommates, who introduced themselves in a jovial manner, and joked around casually while waiting for their meal to be served. There was a tantalizing smell of garlic, beans, and fried onions. The food was brought to the table by a stout, unsmiling old woman called Sitt Haseeba, who thumped down the dishes without a word. Not a charming lady, but she could cook.

There was a strange, viscous, dark-green soup called *mulukheya* that did not appear appetizing, but Channing found it delicious. Big bowls of rice, beans, tomato sauce and coarse pita bread seemed to be just what he needed. Sitt Haseeba considered her work done and left the flat. She was hired by the young men for a couple of hours each day just to prepare the evening meal and go away.

All of his new companions were *tarboush*-wearing, suit-clad members of the educated *effendi* class, assigned to the government secondary school as their first job out of the teacher training college, except one. A heavy fellow, mostly silent—in contrast to the convivial and outgoing manner of the others—called Husni. It took Channing a while to understand that Husni worked not at the school, but at the youth reformatory.

After dinner, they dumped all of their dishes in the kitchen sink and left them there. Ben noted this, and came back later when the common room was quiet, and began scrubbing the pans and dishes.

It happened to be Husni who walked in on him. "What are you doing?" he demanded.

"Just thought I would clean up a bit. Trying to help out."

"What's wrong with you? Sitt Haseeba will do that tomorrow, before she cooks dinner."

Channing found himself unable to explain. He shrugged apologetically and said, "*Ana assif.*" I'm sorry. But then, because he had already committed himself, he went ahead and finished the dishes.

CHAPTER 2

Benjamin Channing and the fresh new twentieth century were born together, in January 1900. The baby arrived on January ninth—so, more than a week later—but he was still one of those for whom personal and public history coincided in a resonant way.

He was born at the family's Beacon Hill townhouse in Boston, near enough to the Harvard teaching hospital in case of emergency. In fact, it was a perfectly uneventful birth, apart from the obvious fact of a new life entering the world. Because it was January, George and Elisabeth Channing felt it was wise to stay in town with the new baby and his two elder siblings until early May, when the warmth of spring was perceptible at the family estate in Blakeport.

In those days, little boys went around in pretty smocks and gowns until they moved up into sailor suits and short pants. Benjamin was a beautiful child, all blue eyes and wispy blond hair, with a creamy complexion and pink cheeks, like the illustrations of toddlers in popular magazines. Elisabeth Channing was not particularly frivolous or vain, but she still enjoyed being seen in public with a child so charming to look at.

Summers were lovely at Blakeport. A cool breeze came in from the sea almost every day. Mrs. Channing would push the baby in the perambulator through the little shopping streets, meeting friends at tea gardens and cafés, walking up and down the long avenue beside the yacht harbor. Mr. Channing spent almost all of his time in New York, doing incomprehensible things with investments and securities, so she was often alone. Mostly alone.

Benjamin was a late and surprising baby in the Channings' life. His brother James was already twelve and his sister Catherine almost ten. Ben became the antidote to his mother's frequent loneliness.

She also found comfort in her faith. Every Sunday in the summer she would take the children to the little St. Giles' Church, a haven of Reformed Presbyterianism in the heart of Blakeport. There was a much more elegant Episcopal church there, and a staid, respectable, prosperous Congregational one. But at St. Giles there was fellowship, and sound teaching, and a kind of attractive humility. Ben's earliest memories were entwined with the sense of feeling fully at home in church.

When the school year began, James went off to board at the Hampton Academy, and their sister to Miss Lorimer's Day School. That made their mother's days even emptier.

She clung to her youngest child a bit until his turn came to enroll at the Hampton boarding school, and at that point, parting was very painful for them both. Benjamin wrote sweet little letters to his mother twice a week.

By the time he was seven or eight, Ben Channing displayed a prodigious aptitude for sports. He loved just about every game he tried, and he had so much natural ability that he easily experienced glorious success. That kind of reward made him even keener to try the next physical challenge.

Benjamin was good at tennis, swimming, running, and golf. He took up specialized track events and medaled in high jump, shotput, and hammer. Then there was wrestling, rowing, horseback riding, and shooting for sport. He tried to join so many teams that he seldom had time for his schoolwork, and Elisabeth sometimes had to limit his extracurricular commitments. So he eventually narrowed down his constant activities to his fondest loves, baseball and sailing, especially in races.

The Great War broke out when Ben Channing was fourteen. The United States was not a formal combatant for another three years, but there was a flood of excitement among certain young American men who saw it as a jolly adventure to find a way into the war.

Ben's big brother James was a Yale grad by that time. Even though the family spent a good deal of time in Boston, they never considered going to Harvard; their legacy extended to Yale's early days, and all of their boys attended as a matter of course.

James Channing and several of his comrades in the Wolf's Head secret society, current students and recent graduates, decided to form themselves into an aviation unit and learn to fly. France was well ahead of the United States in the development of military air power at that time. The aura of glamour that hung over the daring young French fliers was irresistible.

Frederick Trubee Davison—manager of the Yale crew team and a member of Skull and Bones—led what they called the Yale Aero Club, which soon became the volunteer Coastal Patrol Unit #1. About a dozen of them started spending time in Palm Beach, Florida, taking flying lessons while staying at the posh Breakers resort. They learned to service and maintain the tiny aircraft of the time, and they began to lobby the Secretary of the Navy, Josephus Daniels, to begin taking seriously the potential of naval aviation.

Daniels was easy to convince. He was deeply concerned about the new threat of German U-boat warfare and felt the need to expand and modernize the U.S. Navy as quickly as possible.

Before long, the press got wind of this quixotic effort by a handful of wealthy and privileged Ivy League scions, which they promptly dubbed "The Millionaire's Unit." There was an element of mockery in this, but the young pilots didn't care. Publicity helped their cause, and soon the First Yale Unit was a recognized part of the U.S. Navy, drawing in recruits, growing and training, preparing to ship out if and when the United States entered the war. Davison became their squadron leader and was commissioned a lieutenant; seven others, including James Channing, were given the rank of ensign. They practiced target shooting with machine guns installed in their airplanes, dropping unarmed bombs on old boats anchored in the water, and takeoffs and landings on small unpaved airstrips. They learned the ropes of photography and mapping from the air, spotting mines and submarines, and coastal surveillance. It was like another exciting sports activity, only more so.

Young Benjamin idolized his brother James and wished that somehow he could magically be a few years older so he could join them.

But it was at this critical juncture that an unexpected blow struck the Channing family. George Channing, off in New York City, dropped dead in an elevator in his office building. He stepped into the lift in a completely prosaic manner, and when the doors opened on the eleventh floor they found him slain by a heart attack.

James gave up his dreams of flying in the Navy and applied himself to learning the details of the family business in New York.

Their sister Catherine, married and settled in Boston, had existed on the fringes of the family for some years.

And there in Blakeport, the widowed Elisabeth, and young Benjamin, now fifteen, found themselves dealing with the unreal loss of a remote and absent father and a nearly intangible spouse.

"Fairy! How are you, man? So great to see you again!"

One of Ben's friends from the Hampton Academy, now a sophomore, was ready to meet him at Yale when he arrived.

"Ben . . . I don't use that nickname here."

Ben's grin faded, abashed. "Oh . . . I'm truly sorry, Ferrand. It won't happen again."

"That's all right. I'm here to help you move into your rooms. We've got a pretty decent house on York Street with some of the Hampton fellows, and some new men. Just a few minutes from Dwight Hall."

Ben and his friend Ferrand Walton got his things moved into their lodgings at 242 York Street, a fairly comfortable old house with a bit of garden.

It seemed Ferrand knew everyone, especially those in the Student Volunteer Band. Ben was a bit shy in those days, having to push himself to engage socially with others. So it was actually a great help to him to begin at Yale with a gregarious set, all of them interested in learning about missions abroad and evangelizing their neighbors.

He soon discovered that the Student Volunteer Movement members at the York Street house were committed to a conventional Christian rectitude in their daily life. There was no alcohol, ever, at York Street, and they began every day with a half-hour of prayer and Bible reading before breakfast.

They held regular meetings at which they strategized about how best to bring the Word of God to the skeptics and wastrels all around them. They encouraged each other in what was called "personal work"—focusing on a particular individual who seemed receptive, praying earnestly for that person, and seeking openings to raise issues of faith and conscience with him. This approach was new to Ben but he found that it rather suited him, as the prayer and concern turned his attention from himself to the other. He lost his feeling of self-consciousness and began to enjoy encountering new men in classes, at Dwight Hall, and in the numerous sports settings he jumped into.

For the sports culture at Yale was terrific, and he loved it. Competitive, energetic, talented young men threw themselves without a trace of irony into every kind of athletic activity. Ben tried out for several teams for which he was not selected. But baseball was a red carpet for him into social success.

As a skilled pitcher, he stood out right away. Even as a freshman he was placed among the starting lineup. In his sophomore year he was elected captain of the team, an extraordinary honor. Ben was beginning to feel that his place at Yale was assured.

He also performed well enough in his studies to make a favorable impression. He did especially well in languages as he had at Hampton; he chose Spanish and German instead of the classics, with a vague idea that they might prove useful in the future.

Toward the end of his sophomore year, the S.V.M. coordinated a visit to the campus by the famed John R. Mott, leader of the International Committee of the Y.M.C.A. Star graduate of Cornell, Phi Beta Kappa, recognized for his war relief work by President Wilson with the Distinguished Service Medal, chosen as Ambassador to China, author of a stack of influential books, keynote speaker at countless conferences, recently returned from another long fact-finding tour of the Far East. Mott was the kind of man these young students aspired to be.

He spoke to a sizable crowd assembled in the gymnasium, and was warmly welcomed. But while he was speaking, he quoted a passage of Scripture that Ben Channing knew well, but had never really responded to before.

"You accomplished young men," said Mott, "Have many achievements to your credit, and you are only beginning your path through life. It would be easy to rest in complacency on your many advantages and believe that the world will simply produce for you what you desire. But why has God given you the opportunities and abilities you possess? For your own satisfaction? For public glory? Do you somehow merit your place in American society, in the company of nations, in the Kingdom of Heaven? No, my dear friends, I can assure you that nothing of value in your lives has come to you purely because you are entitled to it, least of all your salvation, or your blessed Christian life. The Apostle Paul—who also never earned his unique calling from the Lord Jesus—put it very concisely:

> For by grace are ye saved though faith, and that not of yourselves.
> It is the gift of God. Not of works, lest any man should boast.

Clear enough, that statement, is it not? Hear it, and let it put you in your place."

Mott went on, but Ben Channing did not really hear anything else he said.

After Mott, the campus leader of the Student Volunteer Band, Ferrand Walton, turned the atmosphere of the room from a respectful lecture hall into a rowdy pep rally. He laid out a picture of the imperative manpower needs in foreign missions and the number of unoccupied fields where no Christian presence—at least, of the kind recognized as valid by evangelical Protestants—was to be found.

"Do we study to succeed in our classes? Do we get plenty of healthy exercise in sports and games? Do we get down on our knees and pray, and read our Bibles daily? Of course we do! Because all of these are essential. Body, mind, and spirit, the firm triangle upon which rests a vigorous, robust, muscular Christian life, one that is able to reply when the Master calls for men to serve him, 'Here am I! Send me!'"

An ovation followed these words like a home run on the baseball field. "Is it enough for you to sit in an office all day, go home and read the paper or listen to records on the phonograph, and just wait to grow soft and decayed? Is it? Or do you want to take on a man's job, a tough and demanding job, at which only the strongest will succeed? Do you want to brave the challenges of the most difficult fields in the world, seize the life of daring and achievement, to heed the call and command to bring the Gospel around the world to every living creature? That is the question I ask you today!"

Young men were cheering, clapping their hands, hollering encouragement to each other over the noise in the room, but Ben Channing sat quietly, still thinking about Mr. Mott and his quote from Ephesians. *The gift of God*, he thought. *Not of yourselves . . . lest any man should boast.*

When stacks of pledge cards were passed around the gym, Ben Channing took one. He read, "I am willing and desirous, God permitting, to become a foreign missionary."

Ben looked at this card through a sort of tunnel as if it were very far away. He read it again and again. And then, he signed it.

He felt so doubtful later about what he had done that he avoided Ferrand Walton and the other members of the Student Volunteer Band, slinking around campus by himself until the spring semester came to a close. During the summer vacation he went home to Blakeport.

"So, Mother," he began, as they strolled along the Sound near the yacht harbor. "Have you ever thought about the people around the world who don't know Christ? Doesn't it seem strange that God would call men *here* to go out *there* and help them? An inefficient use of resources, perhaps."

She smiled. "You know that at St. Giles we support several missionaries. Why would we do that if we didn't believe in their work? It may seem that God has chosen a strange way of extending himself to the peoples of the world . . . but who are we to judge his plans? The Bible makes it clear that God calls us to do his work on earth, to be his hands and feet, so to speak. To reach out to others who need help, who are hungry, or sick, or in need of salvation, or of just an act of love, or a word of hope."

"I think some members of our class intend to sign up."

"If God can use them, then let it be so. If they have the skills needed, and the spiritual strength."

"There may be people, though, who would say that a young man in the Ivy League with a successful future ahead of him would be throwing himself away as a missionary. That he's really nothing but a fool."

"There may be people who will share dark counsel, anywhere, at any time."

As they walked at a slow amble, Benjamin held lightly to his mother's elbow. A small affectionate gesture.

"I imagine," Ben said, "That the hardest part of shipping out somewhere would be saying goodbye to one's people at home."

Elisabeth Channing lifted her hand, and pressed her fingertips against her lips. She walked on, turning her head slightly away from Benjamin, covering her mouth with her hand.

When Ben returned to New Haven for his junior year, he had read and studied several current books about world mission, including Samuel Zwemer's *Unoccupied Mission Fields*.

One of the first things he did was add Arabic to his foreign languages. He was a little apprehensive about it, given the fearsome reputation of Arabic as one of the world's most difficult tongues. However, he reasoned that this would be a significant intellectual test. He also registered for courses in world history and religions.

He did not discuss his plans or his misgivings with his S.V.M. or Y.M.C.A. friends. But he did spend more time on his knees, praying about it. He was praying alone in his room when he was interrupted by one of his York Street neighbors, a friendly freckled young man called Patrick House.

"Ben, it's good to find you doing what you ought," said Pat. "But you need to get up and put your coat on. The Lord has need of you."

"What?"

"It's our night down at the Hope Mission, and Jamie Hawley can't come. So you're subbing for him."

"I am?"

"That's the way I heard it. I won't say from where."

New Haven was then a rough waterfront town, where work could often be found on the docks and in the warehouses of the industrial district. It was most definitely not a yacht harbor. Men moved about from the dockyards of Boston and New York through this smaller way-station along the coast, especially if they were sent packing by the police for petty crime or vagrancy; they could relocate by means of a "side-door Pullman" or boxcar on some cargo train, always on the move, never able to settle or support themselves for long.

Also filling the industrial district were the saloons and cheap hotels, the flop-houses, the dance halls and pawn-shops and brothels that sustained this population. And right in their midst was a big old barn of a place called the Hope Rescue Mission.

On the ground floor was a wide meeting hall, with high rafters and plastered walls painted with inspirational Scriptures. The hall was filled with wooden benches and a heavy iron stove. In the front stood a piano and a lectern, and a long altar rail where men could come forward, fall on their knees, and seek salvation.

There was a big kitchen with giant urns of coffee and a few long tables. Upstairs in a little apartment lived Jerry and Agnes McNeill, the patient and long-suffering older couple who operated the Mission.

The doors of the Mission opened every night at eight. A sad and dispirited cluster of men and a few ragged women were always waiting to be allowed in. They headed straight for the kitchen for a cup of hot coffee and a handful of dinner rolls fresh out of the oven. Then they made their way to the meeting hall, where Agnes McNeill led a long session of hymns and songs, traditional tunes that many men remembered from their boyhood, back when life had not yet laid upon them its heaviest burdens. Some sang as best they could, while others sat silently, hanging their heads, and some dozed a little in the room's safety and warmth.

Mrs. McNeill returned night after night to their favorites, including special solos she offered to speak to their downcast hearts.

When I look out on those o'er whom long years have rolled
Whose hearts have grown hardened, whose spirits are cold

Be it woman all fallen, or man all defiled
A voice whispers sadly, 'tis some mother's child.

No matter how wayward his footsteps have been
No matter how deep he is sunken in sin
No matter how low is his standard of joy
Though guilty and ruined, he's some mother's boy.

No matter how far from the right she has strayed
No matter what inroads dishonor has made
No matter what elements canker the pearl
Though tarnished and sullen, she's some mother's girl.

'Tis some mother's child, 'tis some mother's child,
For her sake, deal kindly with some mother's child.

This dose of Victorian pathos was often exactly what was needed, like a pail of water thrown in their faces, to get a reaction from the crustiest cases before her. Groans and the sound of snuffling could be heard in the room along with the music.

The music itself drew in others from the street, and soon the room was filled to capacity. Ben Channing and Patrick House arrived at about that point. It was a long walk from Yale's beautiful campus to this part of town.

Among the dirty and exhausted men and women on the benches were a few restored individuals, clean and sober, properly dressed, who were called there "the converts." The next part of the evening always involved their accounts of personal suffering and redemption.

"Did I look just like you no more than a couple of years ago? Yes, I sure did," testified a man with a shiny bald head, stout and looking strong. "I had work in the lumber yard at Carson's Freight, good work it was, too. But for years I was hitting the bottle, secretly I thought, but no—everyone knew I wasn't pulling my weight anymore, I was so weakened by drink. Sick every morning, puking and sobbing with the pain. Does that sound like you? I don't doubt it.

"So finally Carson's let me go. And without no good report from them, I couldn't get another job. Didn't take long for me to lose my home, since the little money I got I spent straight on drink. I was living on the street, stealing sometimes, begging sometimes. Finally I got work moving coffins from the city morgue to the Potter's Field, burying them boxes unsung and unwanted. I knew for a fact that if I didn't clean myself up, in no time I would end up in a box just like them.

"So I came a-stumbing into this Mission one night, cold and hungry and done to death of myself. I thought it might just be a snap—a way to cheat myself into a warm bed and maybe some breakfast, you know, to work that graft all winter. But these folks weren't fooled. They saw right through me into my barren heart, and they brought me to the Lord in prayer. And praise his holy name, he flooded me with his Holy Spirit, and the drink demon just up and left me. Never have I wanted another drop, not since that night. The smell of a saloon, it sickens me now. The Lord just took it all away. And since that night I been living clean, and working for good pay, and feeling so free, like I never thought could happen. Glory hallelujah!"

Murmurs of praise followed this account. Then a young woman stood up, dressed very modestly in a well-trimmed gown, and spoke in a husky voice to the assembled crowd.

"I could tell you that my life on the street wasn't my fault . . . that I was promised every good thing by a man who dropped me, after I ran off with him and burned all my bridges for him. He just went on to the next girl and I was left with nothing.

"I tried to work in shops and kitchens, and a bakery hired me for a while. But I was drinking too, just like Brother Matthew here, and I couldn't hold a job. And then a certain woman, she told me I could make good money serving drinks to gentlemen at a private club. But I didn't know what she really meant by that. And in no time, I was serving them gentlemen much more than drinks. And this woman, she owned me. It was just around the corner, here, at the Blue Belle, where too many other girls are still trapped in their clutches.

"I tried to run away a couple times, and I used to hide on the street till I got so hungry I would do some kind of business just to get arrested and spend a night in jail. The county jail, on Water Street. It was better than sleeping in a doorway or a dark dirty alley, but not by much.

"And then I came by this Mission. I don't know how I ever dared to walk through that door, knowing what a polluted creature I was. But nobody judged me here. They just loved me, and prayed for me, and somehow the Lord Jesus just entered my heart. And he had the power to change me. And that's the truth, as I live and breathe." With a great sigh of relief, she went back to her bench and sat down.

Ben wasn't sure what he was doing there . . . he simply listened and looked around for a while. Patrick, who had volunteered at the Mission many times, was working the room, talking quietly with any man who wanted attention, praying with some, and just listening to others.

Then came the altar call. Agnes McNeill played gentle music on the piano, while her husband Jerry invited anyone who was in need of prayer to come forward and kneel at the rail. Many did, including four who wept with apparent broken-hearted sincerity and begged the Lord Jesus to save them. Patrick House, Jerry McNeill, Brother Matthew and other volunteers knelt with them, laid hands on them, and prayed with them.

When Ben had finally worked up the courage to do likewise, it was time to feed everyone their supper, so he hurried to the kitchen to help out. He was told to serve the stew into crockery bowls, and this he did with firm dedication.

While the men were finishing their food and they had started cleaning up, Ben found himself addressed by Jerry McNeill, the anchor of Hope Mission.

"I think you're seeing how we live down here, eh? Ever seen the inside of a jail?"

"I've never even seen the inside of a Mission before," answered Ben.

"One reason I like to have young men from the College come down here is for you all to know us as we are, and to witness the saving power of Christ. It's the hopeless and the helpless who are hungry for God. Not comfortable people in steepled churches. I've got to tell you something, my friend: the people who live up on Prospect Street and on the boulevards in great mansions, they are no more to our Lord than these poor tramps and harlots and jailbirds. He has done as much for these as for those who drive through the streets in rubber-tired carriages."

"Yes . . . I believe that's true."

"No question about it. It's just a matter of getting these folks to accept it. To understand that they are beloved sons and daughters of God. Did you notice that there is no fire and brimstone here? These folks do not need to be told about the fall of man, original sin, or endless hell. They already have hell in their own hearts. They already feel drenched and drowned in sin. They need someone to love them, to care about them, and offer them some hope."

It was getting on toward midnight, and many of the men had already been sent upstairs to the dormitories where they could get a night's sleep.

Some had wandered off, and some, not yet ready to receive what the Mission was giving them, went off to the nearest saloon looking for a drink.

Channing and McNeill got themselves a cup of coffee and sat on a bench in the big kitchen. When Patrick had finished helping the men get settled for the night, he joined them.

"You remember what Brother Matthew said about trying to work a snap on us?" McNeill said. "Coming here pretending to be interested in the message just to get a bread-and-bunk? It's funny, 'cause it never works like that. We don't care if they are ready for the Lord or not. We just give. It really don't matter to us. I would rather feed a dozen who are not 'worthy' than miss one who is truly crushed and needing help."

Patrick spoke up at that point. "Feature this, Ben: that supper, for two hundred hungry men, cost about twelve dollars. And tonight, four souls were saved. Can you invest money in one of our aristocratic churches and bring results like that? Three dollars a head, for an immortal soul?"

Ben quickly did the math in his head. Twelve dollars a night, seven nights a week, fifty-two weeks a year.

"It's not just the men as come here that we help. There are families in New Haven without a pound of coal in the house, or a crust of bread, while others take the train into New York City just to shop at Tiffany's for their Christmas presents." Jerry shook his head. "About a month ago there was this young Polack family in the Water Street jail. They'd been shipped from one town to another, nobody welcomed them, no place to live. They were all of them sick. The father got pinched stealing oranges for the kids. We found them a place to stay, with a stove and some coal, brought them soup and bread. But the youngest one was too far gone, and he passed to glory. An innocent babe, done in by the sin of all of us."

Channing knew he should feel sympathy for this suffering family, and he did. But more than this, he felt deeply ashamed.

He began to visit the Hope Rescue Mission about once a week, often with Patrick House, sometimes with other young men. Again he found that, like his "personal work" among fellow students, praying for the other pulled his focus away from himself, and he no longer felt mute and inhibited around them. Many of the men were regular visitors and Ben soon came to know them, learned their names, and gave them the kind of attention they craved.

And almost every time he worked there, he brought McNeill eighty-five dollars, enough for a week's worth of coffee and suppers.

One night, there came into the Mission the most repulsive person Benjamin had ever encountered. They called him the Old Captain, and apparently he had indeed been a respected mariner at some point in his life, working cargo ships along the coast. But now he was one of the "drunkards," those with an addiction to alcohol so compelling that nothing else mattered to them.

He was probably about sixty years of age, but he looked much older, and shuffled his feet with a struggle. A stained gray beard hung down over his chest. He was drooling and his nose was running. His eyes were red, badly inflamed, and rimmed by a sticky substance. Only a few teeth remained in his mouth. He wore a filthy jacket pinned together with a long nail, and instead of shoes he had a bedroom slipper on one foot and a wad of rags tied on to the other. He was surrounded by a powerful and complicated stench, the sum of all things pungent. The other men, themselves often strangers to soap and water, slid down the benches a little distance away from him.

Benjamin sat down beside him—admittedly, sometimes holding his breath—and tried to talk with him. But the Old Captain was incoherent, apparently not even seeing or hearing Ben, but dealing with some grim scenario in his own mind. His hands shook, and he sometimes clenched them into fists.

Ben was a little surprised when the Captain went forward during the altar call. He shuffled slowly to the rail and fell on his knees. Then, turning his face to the ceiling, he shouted out, "Oh Jesus, give me sleep. Dear Jesus, give me sleep. Give me sleep, or I'll die." There was a rumble of sympathy from many of the men in the hall. They knew just what he meant. Addicts in the grip of delirium tremens are deprived of healthy sleep, their minds filled with haunted images they called "the horrors." The prayer volunteers surrounded him.

"He hears you, my brother," said Matthew, laying hands on the old man's shoulders. "Only trust Jesus, and he will give you sleep. Let Jesus help you. Only accept the gift. He will save your soul, and he will give you sleep."

At the end of the service, they tried to get the Captain to eat some of the nourishing stew, but he only managed to swallow a few spoonfuls. And as soon as the kitchen was cleared after supper, Matthew and Ben prepared a big galvanized bath of hot water, peeled away the Captain's soiled rags, and soaked his bone-thin shriveled body in the tub. Matthew tenderly trimmed off his beard and hair, and washed his face like a child's.

They dressed him in old but clean clothing from the charity barrel, and made up a cot for him there in the warm kitchen, because he was too weak to climb the stairs up to the dorm.

"Don't get the wrong idea," said Matthew to Ben. "I don't think this man's been saved, because his mind just isn't clear enough to know what he's doing. He might just take these clothes and pawn them to buy a bottle of whiskey. But he's been helped. And one of these days, he might also be saved. And we're just going to go on helping him as best we can."

"I wonder if he'll live that long," said Ben.

"That's for the Lord to sort out," Matthew answered. "But I'm telling you, one day you may come down here and find the Old Captain clothed and in his right mind, like the Gadarene demoniac. And he may be testifying and praying for others, just as I'm doing now."

One bitterly cold night, Channing had to walk down to the Mission alone, because Patrick House was busy and Jamie Hawley was in bed with the flu, and Ben couldn't find anyone else. He hurried along Water Street in the dark, his hands in the pockets of his warm woolen overcoat.

As he passed a narrow alley, he felt someone take hold of his coat from behind. Turning quickly, he saw a small tattered woman, glaring fiercely at him, showing her teeth. Startled, he yanked his coat out of her grasp.

"What you doing down here, you big swell? Come on then, give me a dollar. Give me an ace, man. Give me an Abe. I could use five dollars." She was dressed in thin scraps, nowhere near warm enough for that weather. She was at that stage of drunkenness when she was angry and full of fight.

Ben hesitated an instant, unsure what to do. He had eighty-five dollars in his wallet, but he didn't want her to know that. He slipped off his warm coat and held it out to her.

"You think I want your castoffs, boy? What am I going to do with that? It's dollars I need, Jack. You high hats go around town with pockets full of cash. You can give me a fiver and never miss it."

Ben put his coat back on and turned away from her; she grabbed onto the back of it again, and they walked down the street that way, like a train car with a caboose. He had a vague idea of leading her to the Mission, where she could get some help.

When they got there, she staggered into the meeting, momentarily confused by the music and the crowd and the bright lights. She tried to sit on a bench but slid off onto the floor, then picked herself up and sat again. She sat for a while, then got up and stomped around, then sat again, all the while making loud rude comments to everyone around her. When Mrs. McNeill perceived what was going on, she unobtrusively stopped playing the piano and moved to intercept her.

"What do you want, you old cow?" the woman yelled. "Why won't anybody give me a dollar? That's what I need. You all talk like a lot of holy Joes, but do you help me with a buck when I need it? Not you. You're a blue nose and a hypocrite. I don't want this. I'm leaving."

Agnes McNeill spoke soothingly to her. "Why don't you just sit down with us for a while? Be quiet and warm. Soon we'll have some supper, and we'll find you a bed to sleep in."

"Don't want your food, don't want your bed. Just want your money to do with it whatever *I* choose."

The woman lumbered toward the door, and Ben began to follow her, but Mrs. McNeill placed her hand on his arm and stopped him. She shook her head, sadly.

But then, once the woman was outside, she decided that the large plate glass window at the entrance to the Mission needed breaking. She began pounding on it with her fists, trying her best to break it, but she lacked the strength in her hands to make it happen.

Looking around, she found a loose brick lying on the ground, and heaving it with all her might, she shattered the window.

Ben was outside in a flash and wrapped his arms around her. She screamed like the souls in hell, fighting and kicking, trying to bite him. "Get your hands off me, you goddam swell! You got no right to touch me! You leave off, goddam it!"

Someone had summoned the police from the nearby Water Street jail, and they arrived with a patrol wagon. It required the combined efforts of Channing and an officer to wrestle her into the van. The vehicle rolled away.

Breathing hard with anxiety and effort, Ben stood thinking about the circumstances of life that might have brought that woman to the state she was in . . . what she had suffered, what might have been done to her. Her vulnerability to alcohol, her small sick body, animated by rage and desperation. Her needy soul. *For by grace are ye saved through faith,* he thought again. *And that not of yourselves. It is the gift of God. Not of works, lest any man should boast.*

The woman continued to snap and snarl for a couple of hours, then subsided into quiet moans and sobs. The police decided to leave her in the jail overnight in the hope that she might be more rational in the morning.

CHAPTER 3

"CHANNING," said Mourad pointedly, "What in the name of the Mighty and Merciful are you wearing?"

They had met on the Tanta station platform to take the morning train into Cairo. Ben looked down at himself, as if his clothes had suddenly appeared on his body without his knowledge. "Is something wrong?"

"If you want to be taken for a bloody British imperialist, then you look just fine."

"Well . . . I brought the kit recommended in Baedeker and Murray . . . I thought that would be all right. We're going to the desert today, aren't we?"

The standard guidebooks for Egypt did indeed have a great deal of advice for travelers unaccustomed to a desert climate. Channing had read these carefully before purchasing his clothing and supplies. He had also read Arthur Brown's *The Foreign Missionary*, and the standard S.V.M. publications on the preparation of candidates for service abroad, and he had taken to heart all of their wise admonitions. Therefore, for this first excursion out of Tanta to visit the Pyramids of Giza with Doctor Mourad, Ben had equipped himself in accord with the best expert advice.

"Are you planning to live and work here, or only to do the sights like a Cook's tourist? Actually, with the itinerary we have ahead for today, you should fit right in, though with the wrong sort of people. But promise me you will never go forth like that in Tanta, or anywhere else in the Delta."

"If you say so."

"And please, at least take off the silly sun-shade hanging down the back of that helmet. You look like your own grandfather. And no parasol, either."

"But . . . they say that the sun is hazardous for those who are not accustomed to it."

"In November? It will doubtless do you good."

Channing remembered what he had read about the desert sun. Great care must be taken to protect oneself from its direct rays, they said. One should invariably wear a cork or pith helmet. Wear one with a long brim in the back, or add to the helmet a cloth sun-shade to protect the neck. It is well, in addition, to carry a white umbrella. Smoked or tinted glasses should be worn to filter the sun's glare upon the eyes. And of course, an entire suit of clothes in white linen or twill was called for. He had even started the day with a cold shower, as recommended.

Mourad continued to evaluate Channing's appearance. "May I ask . . . everything you have on appears to be brand new. Did you bring out nothing but new clothing? Suits, shoes, hats, all of it?"

"I did buy some things . . . didn't have the proper togs . . ."

"It's just that I have never known anyone with an entire wardrobe of new clothes," said Mourad with something approaching distaste.

Ben at last understood the offense he had committed. He looked away and his face colored. "I'm sorry . . . I didn't realize. I think I need some personal advice."

"I'll take you shopping in the *souk* in Cairo. But for now, we need to get on this train."

Benjamin soon forgot his embarrassment in the sheer pleasure of passing through the landscape of Lower Egypt. Just below Cairo, the mighty Nile split into two main courses, one heading northeast and the other northwest, creating a great expanse of lush farmland between them, thoroughly veined with small natural streams and manmade canals. And once a year, the level of the water rose dramatically, carrying with it the fine silt that renewed Egypt's fields with unparalleled fertility. July until October was "High Nile" or inundation season. The broad river flowed with a strong current and filled every irrigation ditch with its precious water. In a land without rain, life in Egypt was literally the gift of the Nile.

The wide and level Delta contained almost no temples or tombs, only farmed fields and villages with their mud houses and date palms like islands rising out of a vast lagoon, reflected perfectly in the still water. The bunchy black oxen of Egypt stood knee-deep in it, waiting to be hitched to plows whose design had remained unchanged since Pharaonic times. In November, the water level had peaked and started to recede, and where fields were uncovered they were quickly sown with the first new crops. Fields of a tall thick clover—essential for animal feed—were already everywhere in their astonishing green, the greenest green possible on earth. The perfect blue of the sky, the extreme green, and in high spots where the water did not reach, a flat dry uniform cocoa-brown; it looked like a landscape a child might color with crayons.

They stopped once in Benha, then continued on to the primary train station in Cairo, a big Victorian mass of iron and panes of glass opaque with dust. Outside the station they stepped into a random moving throng. Countless people passing quickly in all directions, carriages, animals, vendors, soldiers, crowds. Benjamin got only the most confused impressions as Mourad steered him through their midst.

They moved steadily through the Midan Bab al-Hadad and began walking south on Noubar Pasha Street, toward the central Europeanized part of town. The irresponsible Khedive Ismail—he who spent so lavishly on palaces and opera houses and the Suez Canal, plunging Egypt into bankruptcy in the 1870s—was determined to make Cairo the Paris of the East, and in this quarter he nearly succeeded. The luxury hotels were here, the government ministries, the banks, the consulates, the Western-style shopping. Wide boulevards and elegant four-and five-story buildings with French façades, gracious open intersections and impressive churches, all of these were found in the Quartier Ismailiya and nearby. Fine large villas were created there for the Ottoman ruling elite, wealthy landowners, and the city's emerging mercantile class. It was not at all what Benjamin had imagined as the character of Cairo.

Before they reached the landmark Ezbekiya Gardens, there was the famous Shepheard's Hotel, and nearly across the street from it, the substantial buildings housing the headquarters of the American Mission.

American Presbyterians had first arrived in Egypt in 1854, so they had enjoyed several decades in which to do what they did best: they established well-organized institutions in several parts of the country. By the time Ben Channing joined them in 1922, there were over three hundred stable and staffed mission stations, including almost one hundred formally-recognized Protestant churches, served by eighty-three American missionaries and an equal number of trained and ordained Egyptian pastors, plus many more support personnel.

They maintained two highly-regarded hospitals, a new university, and almost two hundred schools, educating thousands of young Egyptian students. Orphanages, clinics, a theological seminary, a publishing house, Sunday Schools, agricultural centers, home-based programs for women and children. The American Mission in Egypt was no frontier outpost, but a major employer, service provider, and social influence in this Arab North African country.

"Here you are, Ben. Just as I promised, I've delivered you to the Ezbekiya H.Q. You should be able to conclude all of your official business here."

"Mourad, thank you! There are several people I need to see, and I have an appointment with Mr. Zwemer at one o'clock."

"I'll be back to collect you at about two, then. I have some things to do in town."

Channing was intending to stay the night at the A.M.E. guesthouse, so he checked into his room and got a key to the building. He went to see a Mr. Prentiss in the administrative office to fill out forms indicating that he was taking up residence in the country, showed them his passport, travel documents, and appointment papers, and had his photo taken for their records. Because Ben had arranged to receive no salary while in Egypt—paying for his own support—they had to create a special category for him, as a voting member of the Missionary Association but at the same time a volunteer.

When one o'clock came, Ben presented himself at Reverend Zwemer's office, where the man sat at a big desk piled high with books and papers. He looked up, unsmiling, but with a polite nod, then stood and extended his hand. Samuel Zwemer was fifty-five years old by that time, the same age as Doctor Philip Hessburgh of the Tanta Hospital, whose opinion of Zwemer hung in Channing's mind. Zwemer was, however, a respected and published authority on the Arab and Islamic world, with years of experience in Busrah and Bahrain before coming to Egypt. He was filling in as head of the Missionary Association while its chair, the venerable J. R. Alexander, was in the United States on furlough.

Zwemer's serious expression, bordering on disapproval, never changed. The face of a kindly man, as he ages, becomes ever kindlier; the face of a severe man, ever more severe.

"Mr. Channing, how fortunate you are to be a young man, arriving at this moment in history at the doorstep of the Islamic world. For Cairo is, of course, the entrance to the world's most resistant citadel of error."

"How do you mean, sir?"

"Well clearly, we are now at the point when the fortress of Islam, defended for centuries by defiance, bigotry, and the weight of tradition, is about to fall. Like all other non-Christian systems and philosophies, Islam is a dying religion, decayed by its own fatalism, neglect of active education, opposition to science, and rejection of religious liberty. For centuries it has accumulated nothing but failure, refusing to awaken and adapt. Injustice and superstition are about to yield to the power of enlightenment; the collapse of Islam is inevitable due to the impact of Western civilization. And you have the blessing of being present at this moment. The closed door is but a challenge to him who has a right to enter."

"Mr. Zwemer, I have read your book *The Disintegration of Islam.*"

"Then you have heard this address before—do forgive me. I seek only to impress upon you the privilege of the calling upon which you are about to embark."

"Thank you, sir."

"I trust you have now recovered fully from your illness?"

"Nearly so, sir."

"Happy to hear that. And I believe you have now had the opportunity to see Mr. Prentiss in the office and make your arrangements. When do you plan to move into the house for new missionaries in Boulaq?"

There was a long and awkward silence.

"The fact is, Mr. Zwemer . . . I am planning to remain in Tanta for the time being. I believe there is a great deal of opportunity for me there, both for learning and for work. I'm due to meet with the Delta Evangelistic Committee next week to explore the possibilities. And I'm already more fluent in Arabic after living with my flat-mates for just a few weeks."

"Flat-mates?"

"Yes, I'm sharing an apartment with six Egyptian fellows, mostly teachers at the government school. During my convalescence. But it's been so successful that I'd like to stay there."

Zwemer's face moved gradually from general disapproval to a much more specific and intense disapproval.

"These men . . . are they Muslims?"

"All but one of them. My friend Wissa Buktur is a Christian. Protestant, in fact."

"Mr. Channing, you *are* new here, and you may not be aware of a few things, and perhaps may be rather easily led astray. You should realize that the Arab is a paradox of good qualities and bad. He is courteous, friendly, patient, brave, and generous to a fault. But he is also devious, argumentative, untruthful, lazy, covetous, and proud. One must be cautious in exposing oneself to his influence."

Benjamin felt a prickle of antagonism sparking through him. He decided that the best thing might be to cut this interview short.

"Thank you for your advice, Mr. Zwemer. I think we'll leave things as they are for now. After a while let's revisit this."

"One moment . . . I plan to go over to Al-Azhar at about this time tomorrow. Perhaps you'd like to come with me. It would be a chance for you to become acquainted with Islam in its inner sanctuary, so to speak."

"Yes I would, thank you. I'll meet you here. Goodbye, sir."

When Ben came downstairs he found Doctor Mourad already waiting. "Listen," said Ben, "I'm feeling a bit depleted. Could we just step across to Shepheard's and get a little lunch? Not sure I'm ready to face the Pyramids without it."

He saw Mourad's face take on a clouded look, but he did not quite understand. "Yes, certainly," said the doctor. "You are still building back your strength, and we've already done quite a bit today. Of course, you should eat."

In a moment, they were across the street and entering another world.

Shepheard's Hotel was the epitome of traveling comfort, where guests enjoyed posh rooms, good beds, thick towels, a soaking bath in huge enameled claw-foot tubs, plenty of soap and hot water. Each room had cold drinking water filtered in stone jugs, fresh dates, and flowers on the table; if anything was lacking, one could open the door of the room and clap one's hands to summon a servant.

The hotel went fully electric in the 1890s, providing lights and refrigeration; it offered its own hair salon, a post office with a franking machine, a bank, and the first office in Egypt of the Cook's Travel Agency. They served Berkshire ham and Yorkshire bacon—in a place where pork was not for sale—salmon from Liverpool, Gloucester and cheddar cheeses, fruit preserves and marmalade, Bass beer. Gentlemen could drink at the beautiful mahogany Long Bar, decorated with rich paneling and huge beveled mirrors, enjoying their Scotch whiskey and Plymouth gin, just as if they had never set foot in a Muslim country.

There were dinner dances at the grand hotels at least once a week; a regimental band played until midnight, when they would strike up *God Save the King*, and be replaced by a pianist for the rest of the evening. These balls were the mainstay of the British residents' social life, along with their exclusive sporting clubs. They provided the ideal venue for what was sometimes called the Eastern Fishing Fleet: the cohort of young women and their mothers going out to the East to meet eligible young officers and British Civil Service functionaries with future prospects, marriage being their objective. Men with orders for India normally broke their long journey in Cairo. Sadly, some young ladies failed to attain what they sought and went home disappointed; these were cruelly known as "the returned empties."

In November, the ballrooms and dining rooms were mainly populated by the long-term British expatriates who lived in Cairo. Those "doing the season" in Egypt filled the hotels from December through March, the ideal time for a journey up the Nile to the magnificent tombs and temples of Upper Egypt. Cook's would arrange their transportation by steamboat and lodging at the hotels there—the Winter Palace, the Luxor, the Cataract—with guided tours of the ancient wonders. Mass tourism from America began in 1925 and turned these excursions into an industry.

Ben and Mourad headed for Shepheard's famous terrace, entered from Kamal Pasha Street, and passed two stone sphinxes moved there from Memphis. They climbed eight steps to the terrace level, some two meters above the street: just right for viewing the panoply of native life without having to take part in it.

The street around the terrace was full of vendors, men and boys trying to sell postcards, newspapers, ostrich feathers, bead necklaces, fly whisks, sugar cane, handmade baskets, inlaid picture frames, roses and carnations. Some more ambitious ones offered live birds or snakes in cages, or a stuffed baby crocodile; often one would see a certain man with a trained baboon dancing to a music-box in a red vest and trousers.

Ben chose a rattan table with two chairs beside the terrace rail, in order to see the street show. Mourad followed him. As they sat down, an Egyptian headwaiter dressed like Mourad in a dark suit and tie with a red *tarboush* gave him a critical glance. Mourad was the only Egyptian on the terrace who was not a member of the hotel staff.

A table full of English matrons in flowered dresses and brimmed hats stared as Ben and his companion sat down. Channing had his back to them and did not perceive their disparaging looks.

A Nubian waiter glided over to their table, moving so smoothly he seemed to be on wheels. He was very dark, wearing a long white gown, a bright red sash and vest, and a red *tarboush*. All of the table waiters appeared to be Nubians—often called Berberines—dressed in this distinctive costume.

"*Mis al-kheir*," said Channing in Arabic. Good afternoon. The waiter merely inclined his head. "What will you have, Mourad? I think I need something meaty. We eat well enough at the flat but I haven't seen any meat yet."

"I have already eaten. I might have a cup of tea, please."

Channing glanced over a small printed menu. "Oh, that sounds good. A club sandwich, please, and tea for us both."

When the club sandwich arrived, Ben could not contain his enthusiasm. "It's delicious," he said while chewing. "Just the right amount of cheese and turkey, ham and bacon. Hits the spot. Sure you won't have some?"

Mourad viewed the ham and bacon with disgust. "Never," he said firmly.

The ladies at the next table continued to stare and whisper. When Mourad could not bear it any longer, he excused himself and entered the hotel lobby in search of a washroom.

The lavish interior of the hotel gleamed with polished marble and brass in a theatrical pseudo-Pharaonic style, with colorful lotus columns and tomb paintings. All of the desk clerks were wearing the *effendi* uniform of dark suit and *tarboush*. Huge potted palms, leather armchairs and Tiffany lamps filled the room. He headed toward the newsstand offering European papers and past it into a corridor where there was a men's room. But at the door stood an *effendi* who looked Mourad up and down, noting his attire; the hotel clerk was in fact dressed much better than Doctor Mourad was and made him look shabby in comparison. Mourad cleared his throat and asked for the kitchens, and the clerk superciliously showed him the way.

When he got there, he announced, "Doctor Muhammad Hassan, Ministry of Health. Sanitation inspection. Show me the kitchen lavatory."

"Yes, *effendi*," said the nearest kitchen worker.

There was a humble facility for employees near the back door. Mourad marched in and privately relieved himself. He immediately felt better. Coming out of the lavatory, he found the same worker waiting.

"How often is this facility cleaned?"

"When it gets dirty, sir."

"Not good enough. You need a firm schedule for mopping and scrubbing all surfaces. See to it."

"Yes, *effendi*."

"And how often do these men wash their hands?"

"By Allah, *effendi*, I tell you, they wash their hands all day long."

"All right, that will do," said Mourad, and left the kitchens.

While Mourad was making his lavatory inspection, Benjamin watched the constant tide of humanity in Kamal Pasha Street, all of the carriages, donkey carts, camels, and an occasional motor vehicle. Eventually, he became aware of the voices of the three or four ladies at the table immediately behind him.

"As I have said time and time again, Patricia, you must have only one Egyptian servant in charge of everything at home. If you have more than one, each of them will leave all the work to the others. You must employ a head Arab, a cook and his boy, and then a gardener, a coachman, and a chauffeur as needed. Then the Arab is accountable for them, along with the cleaners and laundry-women and whatnot."

"We can't all have these wonderful Berberines, though, can we? Not enough to go around. Only enough for Lady Mosby and her set."

"I am sure you do not begrudge Lord Mosby a household appropriate to his station."

"Oh no, of course not," said Patricia quickly.

"Well, as Colonel Watterson always says, you simply want to stand over these people with a stick."

"Not entirely their fault though, is it? The modern Egyptian does not come of a ruling race, but of a race that has long been ruled. Naturally they have not developed strength of character, or manliness, or excellence in work or sport."

"Not to mention that this climate is so conducive to indolence and sloth."

"One could argue that is it partly our own fault as well. The English in our anxiety to be just and gracious toward the coloreds often go too far. The natives respect force and strength and despise weakness."

"After all, the Egyptian is simply not a white man, but a mixture of black and yellow. African and Asian. What can one reasonably expect?"

Ben Channing listened to this conversation, becoming more and more uncomfortable.

Finally, Benjamin got up and went in search of Mourad, finding him on his way back to the terrace. "Time we were leaving," said Mourad. "We need to take a carriage down to Qasr an-Nil, near the barracks. That's where the tram departs for Giza."

At the point where the Ismailiya Canal met the river stood the handsome Italianate structure of the Egyptian Museum, built in 1902. "You must come back here, of course," said Mourad, "but not today." Then there was the very large barracks complex for what the British called the Army of Occupation. An extensive drill field allowed them to conduct training and exercises there. Its location in the heart of the city also served to make a definite statement that was hard to avoid.

Tram Number 14 to the Pyramids crossed the Nile and the island of Gezira, then met the Sharia al-Giza on the western side of the city. In November, the road to the Pyramids formed a cool avenue, eight miles long, lined with shady acacia trees planted by the French, and eucalyptus planted by the British. The raised road stood above the level of the water like a causeway, straight as an arrow, crossing over the irrigation channels. It was a forty-minute trip; before the new causeway and electric tram, the drive could take most of a day.

For the ancient Egyptians, the low fertile valley of the Nile was for the living, while the arid high plateau to the west was for the dead. The mortuary temples, the tombs, the massive monuments forming the Pharaonic legacy belonged to the desert—bare, lifeless, nearly as white as a field of salt. In fact, from the desert came the sodium-based natron that had dried the mummies of the ancestors into imperishable hard leather and allowed them to exist into eternity.

As one approached the tram terminus, the unmistakable outline of the Great Pyramid came into view, but only above and at an angle. One must climb the path to the high plateau or ride on the back of a tiny nimble donkey, picking its way quickly up the long slope on its little hooves, as if on tiptoe.

And when one reaches its base, the overwhelming shape of the Great Pyramid of Cheops, or Khufu, nearly blocks out the sky, looming above as a solid mass of colossal stones of a pale dusty gold, and one begins to understand what all the fuss is about.

Benjamin felt a bit silly riding a tiny beast not much bigger than a dog, but Mourad maintained that it was the best way to make the circuit of the whole Giza plateau and see the two huge pyramids and the third smaller one from all angles. There were camels available as well, but they were chiefly used in posing for photographs. Mourad negotiated with a couple of clever donkey-boys who recognized that they were dealing with a compatriot and not a naïve foreigner. They rode together around the plateau and walked among the enormous structures, examining the supplemental pyramids in the far corner of the level space, the smaller tombs and mastabas and the mortuary temples.

"Are you sure we can't climb one of them, Mourad? Or go up inside? There are a few visitors here doing that."

"I must assume that those visitors enjoy the full use of both of their lungs," said Mourad. "Unlike yourself. I do believe you are not quite ready to undertake that kind of exertion."

"Well . . . Lord willing, I'll be back as often as I can. I've never seen anything like this."

The sun was low in the sky now, and in accord with Mourad's plan, they came at last upon the Sphinx from behind. There was the back of its head, its haunches, its spine, and then they came round upon it from the side and saw its stunning profile. A regal headdress, huge ear, modeled features, chin slightly lifted as if it were looking out over all of the meager business of human life toward something infinitely greater.

One of its giant front paws was visible, while the other lay under a drift of sand that somehow made its leonine bulk even more impressive.

The Sphinx lay in a sort of hollow or depression that the setting sun did not reach; much of its detail was shadowed and hard to see. As they climbed the ridge before it in order to look down on it from slightly above, Ben Channing had a word with his donkey-boy and slipped him some cash. The boy took one of the little beasts and quietly disappeared.

Comfortably situated on the sand, they could now view all three of the largest Pyramids laid out in a row, with the Sphinx crouching below them. But their attention was now drawn to the magnificent sky, tinting itself for a most splendid sunset.

Sunsets in Egypt were legendary, enabled by the vast expanse of sky above the desert, the presence of just enough cloud to catch the light, the exceedingly dry air, and the very fine dust particles hanging in the atmosphere and scattering the sun's rays into their full spectrum of colors. Now the sky to the west put on its evening display. A dazzling turquoise lighted up the horizon, with streaks of ever-changing gold and violet, rose, amber, flaming orange, a tender pink and a yellow blending into pale green. The tallest pyramids held their gold and pink for the longest time, like alpenglow upon snow-capped peaks. Even the most blasé tourist wanting to go back to his hotel could not fail to be struck by their beauty.

The colors in the west became less intense and more delicate, but at the same time the sky above took on the most beautiful deep blue, and a few of the brightest starts began to appear. Ben sighed with satisfaction. "Well, that was just spectacular. Even over the Atlantic I never saw a sunset like that. And look, you can still see so much color . . . lemon, and cantaloupe, and grape . . . celery, pistachio, tangerine, and pomegranate . . . and right there, that's the color of rare roast beef. Or maybe strawberry ice cream."

"All right, I hear you. You're hungry again."

"Well, yes. But here comes little Hussein, right on schedule. *Shukran, ya Hussein*," said Ben to the boy, expressing thanks.

Channing had contrived to send the boy over to the Mena House Hotel, right beside the tram terminus, to buy them a picnic supper. They unpacked bottles of seltzer water, cheeses and sausages, large crusty bread rolls with Danish butter, a box of petits fours, and lots of nice oranges and grapes. Mourad ate everything that he felt sure had no pork in it.

And then, something magical happened. A full moon rose in the eastern sky, as brilliant as any moon could be. It simply poured light on the scene before them, a clear white light that picked out details not seen by day, especially on the crouching Sphinx in its low basin; the enigmatic face leaped into focus—the lips, the brow, the cheekbones, the shape of the jawline and throat—details of its kingly headdress. Individual stones of the massive pyramids stood out, white on their eastern side. The moon's light was bright enough to read fine print.

"Ohhh Mourad . . . you knew this was going to happen tonight, didn't you? You knew there would be a full moon?"

The doctor smiled. "Let me remind you, Ben—Islam has a lunar tradition. At least, our calendar is guided by the moon. What kind of a Muslim would I be if I didn't know this?"

Their evening at Giza was ended by the schedule not of the moon, but of the last tram back to Cairo.

Mourad delivered Ben to the A.M.E. guesthouse and then moved on, saying that he had a friend to stay with in the city. And it was true—someone he always visited while he was there. He walked past the fenced Ezbekiya Gardens, closed for the night, and kept moving past its eastern edge, to an area not far from the European quarter, but of another character entirely.

This was the "red light" district of central Cairo, known as The Fishmarket. The bars and dives popular with soldiers were all packed together in this neighborhood, along with, of course, the brothels. Mourad was heading for a certain house, unlabeled, discreet.

"Madame Yelena," he said to the girl minding the door. She knew that Mourad was expected, and sent him upstairs.

Yelena was his Cairo wife. Not officially, but as a sort of understanding between them. She was from the Balkans—Croatia, she said—and as a white woman in the Fishmarket she served a higher-class clientele. She was special to Mourad, not just any woman. He very nearly loved her.

Mourad kept his promise to take Benjamin shopping, unwilling to be seen with him any longer in his ridiculous desert outfit. He decided that there was not enough time to take him to the *souk*, so they went to a small tailor shop that he knew on the Avenue Ibrahim. He told the proprietor clearly that they wanted only second-hand clothing, and nothing too stylish or posh.

It wasn't easy to fit Ben's broad shoulders. The tailor found him a brown serge suit made for a heavier man, too roomy around the middle, and took some time to alter it until it fit reasonably well. A pair of suspenders helped to keep it together. They bought him a bland bow tie and a slightly scuffed Homburg hat, and soon Ben looked like an Egyptologist on some archaeological site coming into town in search of cold beer and clean sheets.

Mourad also took him for lunch to a tiny hole-in-the-wall with two little tables on the sidewalk, which served the best *koushary* in the neighborhood. This was a wonderful dish, rice with brown lentils and macaroni, covered in fresh tomato sauce and a mountain of succulent fried onions, topped with a big spoonful of creamy yogurt. "Now *this* is food," said Mourad. "Not some effete club sandwich for old ladies." Ben had to agree.

"Benjamin, I know you are going to Islamic Cairo with Zwemer today, and I must say I am uneasy about it. I intend to go there myself and meet you at Al-Azhar. So, assume that I will be there, and please, follow my lead."

"Why? What are you expecting to happen?"

"Let's just say that Mr. Zwemer visits there often and has a reputation . . . he is not the most tactful of persons."

Channing was treated to a lengthy example of Samuel Zwemer's tact in the carriage on the way to the mosque of Al-Azhar. It was a slow trip, for as soon as they left the European quarter and turned toward the Khan al-Khalili, the streets narrowed into the kind of exotic Near Eastern city that Ben had thought Cairo to be. Clogged with foot traffic, fully-veiled women, donkey carts laden with fruit and vegetables, scores of rowdy barefoot children. There was a mosque or *sabil* water-fountain on nearly every street, tall houses with their windows covered in wooden *mashrabiya* screens, projecting out over the street. Ben's eyes could barely take it all in.

Zwemer was giving him the standard lecture on the faults and short-comings of the religion of Islam. The unreliability of *hadith* narratives, the puerile and uncivilized practice of Muslim customs and rituals, the gross lack of chivalry toward women, the opaque nature of the Quran, the many wives and questionable moral character of Muhammad himself—all of these featured in his account. Familiar stuff in Orientalist lore.

Channing's introductory classes at Yale had covered this material, but he did not feel equipped to challenge Zwemer's lifetime of scholarship and study.

What bothered him more was all of the militant rhetoric about battle and victory . . . the danger of Islam infiltrating Africa and Asia, the need to conquer and defeat it, to challenge, to attack, to compete, to dominate, to overthrow. Once his ears had become sensitive to it, Ben heard this kind of language in almost every sentence—metaphorical, to be sure, but offensive and relentless.

"Muslims, as you know, are fanatically opposed to the Christian faith and Western civilization," Zwemer was saying. "They are arrogant, aggressive, and defiant. And nowhere is this more true than at the seat of Islamic learning, the medieval mosque and university of Al-Azhar. They do nothing there but memorize the antiquated and chauvinistic writings of their forefathers, clothing themselves in the rusted armor of the past, taking up weapons dulled by the passage of time, seeking to repel the armies of advancement and truth. Now is the time to besiege them in own stronghold and capture it with unprecedented power."

"Sir, there is something that I have noticed. When we speak of firmness in our own faith, we call ourselves dedicated or committed. But when we speak of Muslims, we call them fanatical or aggressive. There is something about this that does not sit well with me."

Zwemer shot him an even harder look than usual, but did not have time to launch into a rebuttal before the carriage stopped.

They entered at the double doors of the Bab al-Muzayinin and went through the forecourt, past the Library and the school for younger students, into the central courtyard of the beautiful Fatimid mosque, founded in the tenth century. Colonnades with pointed arches formed a large open square, where men stood or sat chatting with each other, performing their ablutions, waiting for the next prayer-time to be announced. The distinctive minarets of the mosque stood out against the sky. Before entering the prayer hall, they were given cloth covers to tie on over their shoes, since Europeans hesitated to go barefoot inside the mosque as everyone else did. They were charged six piastres for this service.

Inside the vast shadowy sanctuary, soft rugs covered the floor. Nine long aisles for kneeling in prayer, one hundred and forty stone columns. Groups of young men sat upon the rugs in groups of ten or twelve, listening to their instructors, who sat with them and read from a book placed on a folding wooden stand. The instructors quietly explained a passage from the text while the students repeated it and sought to learn it by heart. Each sheikh wore a long white gown with a flowing outer cloak in a dark color, a felt skullcap of red or brown wrapped with a white turban, and a long beard of white or gray. Perhaps twenty groups sat working at the same time, but the hall was so spacious that they scarcely heard one another.

Others milling about the room seemed to recognize Zwemer, stopped and talked with him. He had cultivated a relationship with some of the Azharis over the past year or so, donating books to the Library, seeking to debate and discuss Islamic teachings with them. As Ben stood observing, Doctor Mourad quietly stepped in and stood by his side.

Zwemer's pockets were filled with small paper tracts in Arabic, printed by the Nile Mission Press. As he moved along, he distributed these among the students. Mourad took one, entitled *Tafsir Ayat al-Kursi*. Interpretation of the Throne Verse. He read it through quickly, then sighed in an exasperated manner.

Students and others read their copies too, and showed them to one another. There was whispering and a suppressed agitation. Mourad realized that Zwemer was working his way over toward Sheikh Surour al-Zankaluni and his Quranic interpretation class.

The leaflets got there before he did. Sheikh Surour read one and rose up from the floor, grabbed the tracts from the hands of his students and tore them to pieces. He angrily berated the boys for accepting such rubbish, and then turned on Zwemer. "What business is it of yours to come here and claim to interpret the Noble Quran? How can an unbeliever presume to do such a thing?" Following his lead, the students too began to reproach them. The noise disrupted the study hall and brought even more angry faces and voices to encircle them.

Mourad placed himself between several young men and Benjamin Channing. "Don't think *he* is responsible for this. He's just a tourist. He can't even read Arabic," the doctor said. "That other man, he *wrote* this leaflet."

The students turned their wrath upon Zwemer. As soon as their attention pivoted, Mourad put his hand on Benjamin's back and started pushing him toward the door. Ben whispered anxiously, "What are you doing? We can't just leave him here!"

"I think Mr. Zwemer wanted exactly this confrontation," Mourad replied grimly. "Fine, let him take the consequences."

And there were, in fact, some consequences. The sheikhs of Al-Azhar made a formal complaint to the Palace and to the Egyptian government, behind which the British occupiers lurked and did nothing. They had a strict policy in place to avoid stirring up communal strife and therefore did not support the overt evangelization of Muslims.

Mr. Zwemer was asked to leave the country for a while to allow emotions to cool. He spent a nice holiday in Cyprus and returned a few weeks later. But by that time, Benjamin Channing was fully settled in Tanta and no more was said about him joining the others in Cairo.

CHAPTER 4

WHEN little Huda was only five years old, her father the Pasha died. She had no idea that such an important and powerful man as her father could just suddenly stop living. And in the confined, exclusive, proprietary world of an Ottoman harem, there was simply no existence for them apart from him.

Her mother, Iqbal, was a mere girl from the North Caucasus when she found herself in the household of the Pasha—very lovely, very fair. The Ottoman ruling elite in Egypt considered themselves entitled to young Circassian wives. It was such a well-established practice that the uppermost class in Egypt was often called "Turko-Circassian." Whatever they were, it was certainly not Egyptian. They were another foreign occupier in the long, long list of invaders and conquerors who had preyed upon the fading power of the Pharaohs in their dynastic decline, beginning a thousand years before the birth of Christ.

Huda's father, the Pasha, was as Egyptian as the fertile earth, a Sayeedi from the heart of Upper Egypt, near Minya. In fact, he owned a great deal of that fertile earth, more than five thousand acres. Cotton and sugar cane had made him a very wealthy man. He could afford a harem in the Turkish style and a fine villa in the newly developing Quartier Ismailiya in Cairo.

That is where Huda lived, with her lovely Circassian mother, her younger brother Omar, and her father's senior wife, whom she called Umm Kebira, the "Big Mother." The superior status of the first wife was clear. But fortunately she was kind to Iqbal and her children, and when the Pasha died, both women were plunged into deep mourning and stayed that way from that point onward.

Before kidney disease ended his life, the Pasha had appointed a nephew, Ali Shaarawi, to look after his household. The nephew was an adult with a home and a family of his own, so he only visited occasionally to see to the family's needs.

The villa in the Quartier Ismailiya had many large rooms and a nice walled garden full of flowers and fruit trees. And that villa was Huda's whole world.

Huda did not go to school. An ancient sheikh came to their house to teach them the Quran, which she and her brother worked to memorize. Tutors came to teach them French, arithmetic, reading, and writing, and such aristocratic pursuits as painting and piano.

But when Huda was ten years old and began to resemble a woman, this activity ceased. She was never seen outside the private rooms of the house unless fully veiled. Her brother went off to school and experienced the freedom of the city. Huda's life became smaller and smaller.

Once in a while she would go with her mother to visit other ladies in the privacy of their harems. And sometimes, women would come to their house with small articles for sale: clothing, cosmetics, perfumes, hair ornaments.

Winters were unbearably dreary. The villa's nice garden was dormant, and the big rooms of the house felt so empty and cold. They had small braziers full of coal that would keep them warm only if they were sitting huddled over them. To pass the time, Huda and Umm Kebira would place chestnuts on the braziers and wait for them to crack open. Once, Huda set fire to a sheet of paper, just to see what would happen, to attack the tedium of her daily existence. She frightened all of the women of the harem half to death and was severely punished.

That winter Huda developed a fever, and a dismal cold in her head. She became so ill that she could not get out of bed without fainting.

Then, her brother Omar caught the illness as well, and immediately they sent for the doctors, who examined him carefully and expressed much concern. Omar's illness threw the household into a state of emergency. But the doctors left without so much as a glance at Huda.

This was too much for her. Huda's envy toward her brother, his freedom, and all of the attention he always got finally boiled over. She confronted Umm Kebira.

"I'm sick, too!" she exclaimed. "Why don't they care about me? I'm the elder, he's the younger. I got sick first."

Umm Kebira looked at her as if she were ineffably stupid. "Have you lived for ten years without learning anything?" she said. "You are a girl, and he is a boy. The only boy. When he is grown, the support of the family will depend upon him. When you marry, you will be part of your husband's household. Omar will carry on the name of his father and inherit his property. You are nothing to the future of this family, but he is everything."

After that, Huda became gloomy and withdrawn. She spent as much time as possible in the walled garden, watching and listening to the birds in the trees. Two cats lived in the garden and she could sometimes get them to take small bits of meat from her hand, as they paced around staring with their huge eyes.

There was a large glass-fronted bookcase in her father's study, and Huda in her idleness tinkered with the lock until she was finally able to open it. Inside, she found papers in the Pasha's handwriting, which made her grieve his absence from her life. But she also found the world of books. Poetry, philosophy, rhetoric, history, information of all kinds about the world outside her home. Some of it she realized was in Turkish, her mother's native language, which she had learned from her. Some of it was in English or French. She also found books on the grammar of Arabic, the key for her to an ability to read and write the language properly. These books were difficult for her to penetrate, but she was a bright girl, and she had nothing but time.

When Huda was thirteen, she was taking a nap on a hot afternoon when she heard women's voices in the next room. Her mother Iqbal and another lady were having a serious conversation, in a tone not normally used in the harem. "I am empowered to express the interest of the family of the honorable Ibrahim Bashir Bey on behalf of his son Muhammad. They request that I arrange a meeting with you at your convenience."

Huda's mother let a moment of silence go by. Then she said, "I regret that such an arrangement will not be possible. There is already a promise to her cousin, Ali Shaarawi Bey, who is her legal guardian."

"But Madame," the other lady replied, "That would mean marriage to a man with children of his own who are older than she is."

"Nevertheless," Iqbal said. "He is the son of her father's sister and he has the authority to make this decision."

Huda understood what the two women were saying but could not accept that it had anything to do with her. Her mind rejected it. She heard only the word *No No No No* over and over pulsing in her ears.

Ali Shaarawi began to visit Cairo more often, from the family's estate in Upper Egypt. He spent hours conversing privately with Iqbal.

After one of these visits, her mother summoned Huda. In front of her, there was an open velvet-lined inlaid wooden box with stunning jewels lying upon it: a lavish diamond necklace and a matching pair of pendant earrings, in a baroque French style much favored at the Khedival Palace. They were certainly not something that a thirteen-year-old child should have any business wearing. "These are for you," Iqbal said, without further explanation.

Whenever female guests visited them, the jewels were brought out and displayed, until Huda objected that it was vulgar to brandish these items as an exhibition of their wealth.

"Just be happy that you have such a generous husband," one of the ladies remarked.

Her mother's maid and several other serving women began to embroider square pouches of silk with gold and silver thread. These were gifts to be presented to guests on the formal signing of a marriage contract. They also worked on a wedding dress and trousseau.

Two men representing Ali Shaarawi arrived at the house one day. In the presence of her mother, they asked Huda, "Whom do you wish to designate as your representative to sign the marriage contract?"

At last, Huda exploded with anger. "Why are you asking me *that?*" she replied, her voice shaking. "No one has asked my consent for anything at all right up to this moment. Now you ask me something I don't even care about. Just do whatever you want! I can't stop you!"

Extensive work began on the house at once, repairing and remodeling; a separate apartment was created at one end of the house and filled with new furnishings. In the garden, a large festive tent or pavilion lined with colorful appliqué was erected, and strings of lights were hung up all around the villa and in the street in front of it. In the tent were placed two wedding thrones, large carpets, and rows of gilded velvet chairs.

Then came the night when Huda was adorned with her diamond jewelry and a wedding dress thickly embroidered in silver and gold. They were heavy, heavy on her small body. A throng of female guests presented flowers and gifts, shared elaborate pastries and sweets, and enjoyed the performances of musicians and a dancer.

At a certain moment, all of the women were ushered out of the tent, and an opaque veil was lowered over Huda's face. The bridegroom entered with all of the male guests, took Huda's hand and led her to the wedding thrones, where they took their places together. For hours she sat like a wooden doll and endured. Until at last Ali Shaarawi took her by the hand again and led her to their new apartment.

History does not record what else happened that night. But the following day, Huda was shattered to discover that the strings of bright lights and the festival tent were being removed, and it was now clear that her beloved garden had been devastated to make room for the wedding event. The apricot and orange trees had been cut down, the large magnolia tree with its fragrant white blooms was chopped to pieces. The flowering Indian jasmine, the lilies, the fuchias, the luisa trees, and the many abundant rose bushes, all were gone.

Ali Shaarawi stayed in Cairo for only one year, as the two of them lived together uneasily, with much weeping and anger. He spent more and more time away from the villa, until finally they were told that he had returned to his wife and daughters in Upper Egypt. Huda felt nothing but immense relief.

Her husband stayed away from her for seven years. And Huda was able to use that blessed interval to grow up.

She had an income of her own of fifty pounds a month, derived through her inheritance from her father. Under Islamic law, that money belonged to her alone, and she could decide what to do with it.

She hired a new piano teacher and an artist to train her in drawing and calligraphy. She tried to employ an aged sheikh from Al-Azhar to teach her Arabic composition and grammar, but was unable to find one who was willing to come to her house merely to instruct a girl.

A very lucky star somehow brought her a wonderful French tutor, a Madame Richard, the widow of an irrigation engineer, a charming and sympathetic woman. Huda had exhausted her father's small library, but Mme Richard had access to unlimited literature in French. Together they read novels and poetry, history and biography; they studied painting and architecture and music. Mme Richard gave Huda her own copy of the Larousse dictionary. Huda began to keep a personal journal in French.

Together they attended performances at the Khedival Opera House, going through the hidden entrance and staircase reserved for women and sitting in the special boxes screened by grillwork where they could listen but not be seen. Huda would leave the house wearing full Turkish dress: the enveloping black *izar* over her clothing, a *tarha* covering her head, and a long white *yashmak* veil over her face. But leave the house she did.

She attended seminars at the university, where a lecture hall was made available on Fridays exclusively for women. Speakers presented research of many kinds, especially in current political and social thought, under the patronage of the Khedival Princess Ain al-Hayat.

With her and with other aristocratic women, Huda supported a charity known as Mabarrat Muhammad Ali. This effort included a clinic and dispensary for the poor, and a school for the training of uneducated women in child care, home management, health and hygiene, and basic literacy. Charity work sponsored by Lady Cromer and undertaken by American and European missionary groups served as the model for this exercise in *noblesse oblige*.

Through Mme Richard, Huda began to attend the literary salons held at the home of the eminent Eugénie Le Brun, where women gathered to discuss essays and articles by Egyptian thinkers of the day, available in French. Huda discovered the work of the Al-Azhar sheikh Muhammad Abduh, a prominent Islamic reformist who had started to argue in favor of increasing rights for women. And then, a book appeared by a lawyer called Qasim Amin, *The Liberation of Women*, in 1899. This book was immediately the only thing discussed in intellectual circles and created a fierce backlash as well as strong support.

The obvious parallels between the subjugation of women and the powerless position of their country under foreign occupation shook the world of Egyptian secular nationalism. "For generations our women have continued to be subordinate to the rule of the strong, and are overcome by the powerful tyranny of men," wrote Qasim Amin. "Men have not wished to consider women as anything other than beings fit only to serve men and be led by their will. Men have slammed shut the doors of opportunity in women's faces, thus hindering their development. As a consequence, the only recourse left to a woman is to be a wife or a whore."

Huda could feel her soul being broken open by these words.

She had become a sophisticated and cultured young woman, twenty-one years old, when her husband Ali Shaarawi suddenly re-entered her life. He was now a Pasha in his own right, active in nationalist politics, ready to relocate to Cairo, and apparently fed up with the life of a feudal lord in a rural backwater. Imagine his surprise when he found he had a wife who was more than his intellectual equal, poised and well-connected in society. One hopes that he learned something from that experience.

Before long, Huda had borne him a daughter and a son. She was an attentive mother, but that did not stop her engagement with public life.

Both Huda and Ali Shaarawi poured energy into the nationalist movement. They became close friends of Saad and Safiya Zaghloul, key organizers of resistance to colonial occupation. Saad was a judge who had served as Minister of Education, and then in the Ministry of Justice; Safiya was the daughter of a former Prime Minister. In 1913, Saad became a leader of the Legislative Assembly, a powerless body that nevertheless gave him a strong platform to be heard in political circles and the press.

The Great War only intensified nascent Egyptian nationalism. The British occupiers declared martial law, and troops poured in both to protect the Suez Canal and to use the country as a staging and supply point, especially in the Delta. They requisitioned huge amounts of food throughout the Nile Valley, animals and animal fodder, and almost the entire cotton-seed crop for edible oil, even date-palm trees to be used for fuel. Villages began to suffer food shortages; there was a sharp rise in hunger and disease. There were shortages of rice, beans, poultry, even onions, and prices tripled. Workers began to be impressed into the Labour Corps, especially camel drivers; there were not enough horses, mules, donkeys and cattle left in the countryside to do necessary farm work.

People in rural areas began to resist, first with strikes, then with targeted violence. They attacked the railways and trucks used to take away their goods. In solidarity, students and workers in the cities staged demonstrations and strikes. Pro-Ottoman foreigners and known Egyptian nationalists were arrested and accused of stirring up the anti-British reaction.

In this tense atmosphere, the Paris postwar peace conference in 1919 was seen as a means of presenting the cause of Egypt's freedom to a world assembly. Saad Zaghloul, Ali Shaarawi and some of their associates demanded the right to travel to Paris as a *wafd* or delegation, to call for an end to both Turkish hegemony and British occupation in Egypt. They seized upon the Wilsonian concepts of popular sovereignty and national self-determination to support their cause. But Sir Reginald Wingate, then the British High Commissioner in Egypt, gave them a flat *no*.

At this, chaos erupted all over the country, and Cairo was paralyzed. Widespread strikes closed the schools, courts, transport, and businesses. People flooded into the streets to protest the decision; Huda Shaarawi and Safiya Zaghloul organized a Wafd Party female auxiliary and staged marches of angry women, an effective tactic because police and the Interior

Ministry were unwilling to accost or arrest them. Saad Zaghloul was seized and deported to Malta. In response, the demonstrations became far more desperate and violent.

Huda used the network of female contacts she had built to call women into the street. They gathered at a park near Qasr an-Nil and planned to move toward the British and French legations; they marched—wrapped and veiled—carrying placards that read *Down with Occupation* and *Long Live Justice and Freedom*. Students and other activists formed columns beside them. But when they reached the home of Saad Zaghloul, the street was blocked by British troops who quickly surrounded them.

Huda Shaarawi, in the front of the crowd, stepped forward, and the troops trained their guns upon her. She shouted, "Let me die so that Egypt will have a martyr!" This standoff ended hours later without any shooting, but others did not. Egypt did have its martyrs, and funeral processions for them only led to greater anger and violence. Everything the British did to repress the marches and demonstrations had the opposite effect.

Recognizing their error, the British removed Wingate and replaced him with General Allenby, hero of Palestine, and released Saad Zaghloul from exile.

They then publicly renounced their Protectorate in Egypt and proclaimed Egyptian national independence as of March 1922. A Constitution and a new electoral system were to be created, separate from the collapsed Ottoman Porte, with Fouad I as Egypt's King. This canny political move settled the popular disorder for the time being, but did nothing to change the power dynamic in Egypt, for the British had reserved to themselves all of the essential functions of state control: national defense and foreign relations, internal security, the protection of all British imperial interests, the Suez Canal, and the Sudan. It was independence in name only.

A manifesto denouncing this sham independence was prepared, calling for rejection and resistance. All of the signatories of this document were arrested, convicted, and jailed.

When Benjamin Channing came to Egypt in October 1922, all of this nationalist fervor was bubbling just beneath the surface. Seldom did they get through dinner at the apartment where Channing lived with his flatmates without extensive discussion of the issues.

"I heard today that the women have gathered again, at the Cathedral of Saint Mark," said Wissa Buktur. "They are demanding that the Prime

Minister resign. And the rumor is that his own wife is going to force him to do it."

"My father works at the Central Communications office in Cairo. The women went there and offered their gold jewelry to the heads of families to get them to go out on strike. Those men have already been without salaries off and on for two years. Many of them are so afraid for their jobs that they have signed letters promising not to strike."

"Where would they work if they lose their jobs? We all know that the Egyptian *effendis* in government service and banks and offices are powerless. If they let out one squeak they are punished."

"Their bosses are all Brits or Turks or men with a lot of personal connections, even if they are no good at their jobs. They get promoted while Egyptian workers get fired."

"We all know that's true. My father says his boss doesn't even know how to send a telegram."

"I heard something else today," said Abbas Bahri. "Do you remember that British professor at the Faculty of Law who was shot in the street? He didn't die, but he couldn't identify the person who shot him. There was evidence, though—the shooter lost his *tarboush* at the scene. They arrested a whole lot of men, just anyone probably, and they made all the suspects try on the *tarboush* to find out which one did it. But the attacker had just cut his hair short, so the *tarboush* was too big for him." The young men laughed.

"Did that really happen? It sounds like a joke," said Ben.

They laughed again.

Ben Channing also talked politics with his friend Doctor Mourad, and because they could discuss the issues in English, Ben understood it better.

"So, it's clear that there are plenty of reasons for people in Egypt to be upset," Benjamin said to him. "It reminds me of the American Revolution against the British . . . fighting the Redcoats at Lexington and Concord. Dumping tea into Boston Harbor, and all that. But here, I can't really see who is in charge and where it's going."

"You might say that it's a colonial uprising and a class struggle at the same time. The *fellahin* or peasants in the countryside—they are angry about losing their animals and crops, and having all decisions about irrigation and water use made by British engineers. The Wafd Party is made up of the uppermost class of wealthy and dominant families, the Pashas, who believe they have the right to rule. And then there are the people like me, the *effendis*: lawyers, teachers, government clerks and lower managers, medical men, the educated and Westernized professionals. All of them have their reasons, and it appears to me that no one is in charge."

"Why are the *effendis* part of it? They are the ones who keep the imperial machine going. Without them the British bosses couldn't accomplish a thing."

Mourad looked sour. "Yes of course, they depend on us for everything. Yet we are paid pitiful tiny salaries and have no advancement opportunity. The laziest university blokes fresh out here from England have authority over skilled and experienced men old enough to be their fathers. They exploit and humiliate us. Why do we serve them? That's a good question."

"And the answer is . . . ?"

"We too must eat. We must have an apartment somewhere. Perhaps one day we can even afford to marry. But to establish a private medical practice for a consulting physician, that takes capital. Thousands of pounds. Unless you have family money, it's impossible. So, you go to work for a hospital and live on the tiny wages they pay you, and you have no other choice."

They were having a thick sweet Turkish coffee in tiny hourglass-shaped glasses, at a downscale café near Tanta's Cotton Exchange and the Courthouse. It was a mild afternoon in January with just enough sunshine to sit at a table outside.

As they were leaving, Mourad spotted a paper notice stuck to the wall, announcing a meeting at the café that evening with a guest speaker, the founder of an organization called the Hassafi Welfare Society. His name was Hasan al-Banna. The name rang a bell with Mourad, and he decided on the spot to return that evening and hear what the man had to say.

Shortly after the evening prayer, the large space inside the coffee shop began filling up with men, many of them young, most of them in the typical *effendi* garb of dark suit, white shirt, dark tie and red *tarboush*. The speaker looked just like them. Before he began to speak, the room was full, with many listeners standing along the walls. Mourad wondered how many of them were police informants.

"Brothers," the young man addressed them. "I saw some of you at the mosque tonight, doing your duty. Tell me, did you come away from prayer with your head held high? Did you feel the power of our faith, the noble truth of Islam? Did you? If you did not, the fault is not entirely your own. The fault lies in the faint shadow of itself that Islam has become, in the land of Egypt. The most perfect revelation of divine truth, the revelation that once rescued Egypt from the filth of paganism, from the rubbish of polytheism, from the mind and heart of deadly ignorance, the *jahiliya*. Where is the power of Islam today? Where is its eternal glory?"

Hasan al-Banna had gripped the attention of his audience right from the start.

"I look around at you, brothers . . . I see myself in you. I too am a teacher, trained at the Dar al-'Ulum, assigned to a school in the Delta to serve my country. I am not a white-bearded scholar in the halls of Al-Azhar, endlessly repeating the same ineffective rhetoric and counsel of resignation to the error and atheism of our age. They have lost touch with us, the young and the inspired, who are ready to combat the wickedness of our present world.

"What's more, they have lost touch with the flawless leadership of the Prophet and his Companions. They no longer follow the righteous *salaf*, the ancestors, the original teaching and practice of the first age of faith. They are weak, they are compromised, they are submissive to the powers of colonialism that control our country! We cannot look to them to lead!"

There was a reaction from the crowd to these words that felt to Mourad like a shudder of fear. The sheikhs of Al-Azhar were closely monitored by the government and expected to do their part to maintain order in the land; their position was significant, and powerful. Criticizing them openly could be dangerous.

"What can explain the weakness and decline of the Muslim world? It must be because we have abandoned the old way, the way of obedience. We have become lax and shallow in our faith. We must renounce all alcohol and food that is prohibited. We must fast precisely, pray diligently, give alms generously. We must abstain from unlawful relations with women. We must keep our wives always in holy submission, separated from men. We must save money responsibly, shun laziness, and stop hanging around in coffee-houses." At this the men listening gave a nervous laugh.

"We must use only Egyptian products, not chasing after foreign luxuries. We must give up gambling and other forms of wasting time and money. We must raise our sons properly to be true Islamic leaders, and our daughters to be pure vessels for the next generation. Are we doing all of these things? Are we?

"Above all, my brothers, we must reject the presence of the occupiers, who shame us with their power. We must expel them, and their servants the Christian missionaries, who denigrate our faith and try to steal the loyalty of our children from Allah. You who claim to be Muslims, how can you send your child to a Christian school? If you look right over there, across the canal, you can see the beautiful school of the Catholics, the Saint Louis College, and their big church. Do you send your son there to become a fine European gentleman? What devil has deceived you?"

Doctor Mourad, graduate of Asyut College, product of a Christian missionary school, felt distinctly uncomfortable.

"How did these wicked foreign people conquer us? It was not only the failure of our weak and foolish leaders. It was the failure of the people as well, because we allowed them to do it. We fell away from the straight path. What does the Noble Quran tell us, in the blessed Sura *al-Qitaal*? 'If you turn your backs on Allah, He will replace you with another people who are not like you.' That is what happens if we withhold ourselves from Allah.

"When we Muslims held firmly to the teachings of Islam, we conquered and reigned over the world. We were wealthy, and powerful, and free. The righteous ancestors bent their necks to no man. Islam is meant to rule and all others to submit. But we denied our religion and ceased to follow it. We became weak and decadent, and we will remain in this state until we recover our strength in obedience." Hasan al-Banna's voice rose to a shout. "Rise up, O my brothers! Eject imperialism from your souls and it will leave your lands!"

There was much more in this vein. Some of his hearers seemed quite moved by the speaker's words and uttered exclamations of approval and support.

Some persons who appeared to be associates of the speaker moved through the room, picking out receptive young men, taking down their names and other information. At that point, Mourad decided to slip out into the night.

He walked beside the al-Qasid Canal past the Collège Saint-Louis and the church of the Pères des Missions Africaines. These were indeed fine buildings, large and handsome. It was a clear winter night, chilly but still, and the reflection of the brilliant stars sparkled in the water. A delicate crescent moon floated above the spire of the church.

Mourad knew that these Catholic institutions were sponsored and supported by the French government. And France was a colonial power. Did that make the work of the school illegitimate?

And what about Asyut College? The American schools were not a function of the United States government, nor were any of their staff salaried by it. He remembered well the diligent work of the teachers and their concern for and interest in the students, which Mourad had felt was genuine. They gave him a first-rate secondary education in the sciences, the best available in Egypt at the time. And because he had no intact family to support him, they did not even make his poor mother pay school fees; she could barely feed her children by working as a laundry woman at the Asyut Hospital.

Certainly, they were not without their flaws. And true, they had made him take Bible classes and learn about the Christian faith. But they seemed to be doing their best to educate and serve the young people of the country. Were they actually just trying to steal them away from the House of Islam? Was Asyut College nothing but a Trojan horse full of Egypt's enemies?

He walked on along the canal, past the Catholic convent and girls' school. Before the missionaries came, there was no schooling at all for girls in Egypt. Almost all women were uneducated and illiterate—all but one or two percent. He remembered his father saying, "A book in the hand of a girl is like a knife in the hand of a monkey." Yet the European and American teachers valued girls as they valued boys. By teaching them, they proved that girls could indeed learn and excel in the classroom and the professions, if only given a chance.

Hasan al-Banna would keep girls and women enclosed in the harems forever, with nothing to do but give birth to boys. Was that really all that God intended for them?

Mourad kept walking until he got to the Tanta Hospital, where his small apartment was found. The American Mission did not pay him well, but it did provide his modest lodging. And the money to pay his salary came as voluntary gifts from the pockets of ordinary Presbyterians back there in America. Why did they care enough about sick people in Egypt to pay him to treat them? What did they gain by it?

And what about a man like Dr. Philip Hessburgh? He had devoted his entire career to alleviating the sickness and suffering of a people who were not his own. Was he really just an imperialist in disguise? Mourad could not bring himself to believe that.

He could believe it, however, about a man like Samuel Zwemer. Zwemer and Hasan al-Banna were combatants, competitors, trying to win souls in a contest for global power. Frankly, Mourad could not see a piastre's worth of difference between them.

It was late when he got up to his room; he was tired and hungry. He ate an orange, then began to undress for bed. Then he stopped himself, and went to the sink and turned on the tap.

He said aloud, "*Bismillah.*" In the name of God. Then he washed his hands, rubbing between the fingers, three times. He cupped his right hand to hold a little water and sucked it into his mouth, swirled it around for a moment, then spat out the water into the drain. He also rinsed his nostrils. Then he washed his face with his hands, stroking water from the hairline to the chin, then from ear to ear.

As he washed, he thought that Hasan al-Banna was right about something: Mourad did not pray consistently, as required. Interrupting the work of a hospital physician to pray five times a day was inconvenient. But he doubted that Allah would find this an acceptable excuse.

He washed his right arm under the tap, up to the elbow; then, the left arm. Using his wet hands, he stroked his head from the hairline to the nape of the neck, and back again. He cleaned his ears with water. Then under the tap he washed first his right foot and toes, then his left foot, up to the ankles.

He pulled out his small prayer rug from under the bed and unrolled it. Standing on the little rug, he recited, "*Allahu akbar . . . bismillah ar-rahman ar-raheem . . . alhamdu lillah irrabb il-'alameen . . .*" He bent forward with his hands upon his knees, stood up again, and then knelt down and pressed his face and hands against the rug. He rocked back on his heels, then pressed his face forward upon the rug again. He completed one *rakaa*, then went through the process again, performing four *rakaat*. That was *'ishaa*, the night-time prayer.

He had to admit that he felt less fatigued and anxious, more calm, more blessed. This feeling lasted until he undressed, climbed into bed, and dissolved himself in sleep.

CHAPTER 5

Sunday, 14th of January 1923
8:00 p.m.
Tanta

M<small>Y</small> dear Mother,

I have not received a letter from you since I got out of the hospital, which is very painful, but I am sure it is not your fault. There has been some civil disorder here that is causing frequent strikes and disruptions. I imagine that there are several letters from you in a box under someone's desk at the Post Office waiting to be sorted.

It's more likely that you are getting my letters, because we can often send them with someone who is traveling to the United States or Europe who can mail them there, bypassing the Egyptian postal system. You must know that I was thinking of you all having Christmas together in Boston, with Catherine and her children, and maybe James as well. I hope the little ones enjoyed whatever it was you bought for them as gifts from Uncle Benjamin!

We had two Christmases here . . . first on the 25th of Dec at the St Andrew's Church in Cairo, and then on the 7th of Jan at the Egyptian Protestant church here in Tanta. They observe the Coptic Orthodox holiday because so many of their family members are still Orthodox, I guess. Some missionaries here believe this is evidence that the Egyptian Protestant church is not sufficiently Reformed. But maybe they are just looking for something to be critical about. I find the Christians here to be gracious and brave, enduring much discrimination for their faith. My friend Wissa Buktur and I worship together every Friday morning, because Sunday is a school day and he must work. Friday is mosque day for Muslims and they take precedence here due to their numbers, of course.

Another of my companions at the apartment called Husni is indirectly responsible for a new ministry in which I am engaged. At least, I hope it will be a ministry. He works as a teacher at the youth reformatory here. It's actually called the Tanta Industrial School, but everyone knows it's a kind of jail. Adolescents and even younger boys are remanded there for petty crimes like vagrancy and theft. The thing is, they are not actually tried, or given a specific sentence. They are simply sent to the school to get straightened out, take basic classes, learn a trade, and then get discharged in an improved condition. It's a delinquent home, really.

I used to watch the boys from my balcony at the Hospital and they seemed so dispirited. My heart went out to them. They are rather like the poor folks at the Hope Rescue Mission in New Haven, just off on the wrong foot and needing help.

So, I have started volunteering there, spending time with the boys and especially leading some sports and other fun activities with them. Many of them want to learn a little English, to annoy tourists, probably. They are teaching me a great deal of Arabic but I have to take care that it is not the kind of language one cannot use in polite company.

The Director of the reformatory—he calls it a "Borstal"—is a rather strange British gent named Fauber, very talkative, full of theories about modern ways to accomplish youth reform. I gather that the first Borstal Institute was founded in England some twenty years ago, mainly to separate young offenders from adult prisoners and to try to rehabilitate them before they grow up to be hardened criminals. They progress through several grades, gaining more privileges with good behavior and reaching certain learning milestones, until they are allowed to join activity clubs, go on outings and so on. That's what I am meant to help with.

You will be happy to know that I am feeling quite well now. My friend Doctor Mourad is taking good care of me. He says my lung is nearly healed. He won't let me hang about near men who are smoking cigarettes, which seems reasonable. The big challenge here in the winter is somehow staying warm in our apartment. Buildings here are designed for hot weather, with very high ceilings, thick walls, big rooms, tall windows, surfaces of cold tile and plaster. In the winter Egyptians wear layers of wool, wrap their heads, and complain a lot. I am writing to you now at my desk wrapped in a blanket from the bed, wearing my "long johns" and several pairs of socks.

Everyone thinks of roasting in the Egyptian desert but not of chilblains and shivering in the cold.

I hope you are taking proper care yourself in snowy Boston. Please know that I love you dearly and never stop missing my home. Blessings to Catherine and the tykes. With my fondest love—your son Benjamin.

They met in the Egyptian Protestant church at Tanta, one of the two formally organized Presbyterian congregations in Lower Egypt. Together, they constituted a subset of the Delta Evangelistic Committee. The full committee met only twice a year, due to the time and expense of travel for people posted in Rosetta or Port Said and the like. But every six weeks or so, the members of the American Mission in Egypt for the Gharbiya Province got together to pray, plan, and discuss their ministries.

"Will the meeting come to order, please?" said the Reverend Peter Reed, chairman of their subcommittee. "Let us open our meeting with prayer. Almighty God, who of thy great mercy hast gathered us into thy visible Church; grant that we may so honor thee, both in spirit and in outward form, that thy name may be glorified in us, and that we may be true members of thine only-begotten Son, even Jesus Christ our Lord. Amen.

"Mr. Channing, I believe you are taking the minutes. Please show that present are the Doctors Hessburgh and Grant, the Reverends Reed, Walker, Acheson and Baird, the Misses Finney and Bostram, and yourself. Right, then. Is there any business outstanding from our last meeting? Any corrections or additions to the minutes?"

"Pardon me, Mr. Reed . . . I notice that the Tanta Hospital nurses are not here, Miss Tate and Miss McCaul," said Ben. "Should I mark them as absent but excused?"

"Yes, if you please, Mr. Channing. Let us begin with the report for this quarter on the native evangelists. You see before you the current list of A.M.E. employees for the Gharbiya Province. It shows each man's name, salary, and rent, place of residence, size of family, and a brief assessment of his effectiveness as reported by a missionary associate. As most of you know, the normal practice is to begin with a salary of four Egyptian pounds per month for a beginner, who joins us with a minimum of two years' work in secondary school, normally in Asyut. He may receive an increase every year of fifty piastres until reaching the sum of six pounds per month. They normally start with a rent allowance of one pound."

"But, Mr. Reed," interrupted Miss Bostram. "It says here that Gergis Stefanos in Menufiya has a rent allowance of two pounds, and is requesting a rise to two pounds fifty. That seems a very high rent indeed. And his rating of effectiveness is shown as merely 'fair.' I wonder whether that is a justified expenditure."

"That is correct, Miss Bostram," replied Doctor Grant of Menufiya. "But you see, it also shows that he and his wife now have four children. They need a larger dwelling than a young man right out of secondary school. Also, he is our senior native evangelist and fills in for the two young ones, Mikhail Abd al-Masseh and Salib Faris, when they itinerate with me in the countryside. I would say that the demands of his growing family and stretching to do the work of three men perhaps impairs his effectiveness."

"Not sure why we must tolerate that," sniffed Miss Bostram.

Mr. Acheson suggested, "Perhaps we should postpone the pay increase for rent until there is a perceived improvement in his performance. As an incentive."

Doctor Grant sighed, but did not contest this statement.

"Are there any further comments or questions about this current list?" asked Mr. Reed. "I can report that Shehata Elias and Awadullah Yusuf here in Tanta are doing reasonably well, as are the two men in Kafr as-Sheikh. Would you agree, Mr. Walker?"

"Yes, for the most part. Sayf Basilios is a particularly good preacher, and I hope he will pursue further training at the Theological Seminary soon."

"Thank you, everyone. May I have a show of hands to approve this report? Thank you."

"Oh, I beg your pardon," said Mr. Baird. "I meant to report that our native evangelist in Danasur village, the one who died last year . . . we have arranged to move his family to Tanta so his daughter can attend Miss Bostram's school and his widow can participate in the training program for Bible Women led by Miss Finney."

"Yes, isn't that wonderful!" said the friendly, smiling woman with the unlikely name of Minnehaha Finney. "Lovely lady she is, too, and very devoted. She has taken to the work like a duck to water."

"Delighted to hear it. Now, I believe Mr. Acheson and Mr. Baird have a report on the distribution of tract literature from the Nile Mission Press."

"Here is a page showing the specific titles we have approved for use in this district," said Mr. Baird. "There are perhaps a dozen Scripture portionettes, ten pamphlets meant for Muslims in particular, and another five titles to stir up Christians to greater zeal. We have found each of these to be filled with sound teaching and generally well received."

Ben Channing read the list, and saw that one of the titles was *The Throne Verse*—the pamphlet that nearly caused a serious incident during his Al-Azhar visit with Samuel Zwemer. He considered bringing that up, but decided against it.

"I believe Mr. Walker has made progress on the training manual for Muslim inquirers, and those preparing for baptism. Am I right about that?"

Mr. Walker replied, "We have a draft that I would like to circulate for your study and comment. I've been working on it with the two native evangelists in Kafr as-Sheikh. The title is *Requirements for Baptism and Preparatory Course of Study for Muslim Applicants*. I have been meeting with several candidates twice a week for several months, going through the course of study as a sort of test run. Perhaps when we meet in March or April we can discuss it."

"Easter is on April first this year, and then there is Coptic Easter, so we may not meet again until late April or May. I'm proposing April 23rd or the following week."

"That's fine. We will still have time to make edits before the meeting of the whole Delta Evangelism Committee in June."

"We have one more item on our agenda that I am aware of," said Mr. Reed. "No, actually two. First, Doctor Grant and I are planning an itineration in the houseboat *Allegheny*, beginning as soon as we can make all preparations. It has been a bit more difficult to provision the boat since food and fuel prices are so high just now, as all of you are well aware. We expect to take her down the Mahmudiya Canal to the villages below Kafr as-Sheikh. Mr. Channing, we'd like to invite you to come with us on this itineration. Get to know the Delta, see the village work for yourself. Would that be agreeable to you?"

"Mr. Reed, I'd love to do that. Thank you! I'm a little concerned about my absence from the work at the school, however."

"That is, in fact, the other agenda item I meant to raise. Can you give us a report of your involvement at the Industrial School?"

"Well, as you know, I've only just started there a few weeks ago. Still trying to establish some trust and comradeship with the boys. They are naturally quite skeptical of anyone they see as a figure of authority. So, right now I go there and mainly run and kick a ball around with them. I've taught them a simple kind of flag football—no tackling allowed—in which players wear a belt with scraps of cloth on it and the defender must snatch a flag to end the down. They quite like it."

"Perhaps because it involves stealing something," observed Miss Bostram.

"I don't like to disappear suddenly just as we are beginning to know each other. But if I have a week or two in advance, I can perhaps prepare them."

Minnie Finney gave him a sympathetic look. "You are right to be concerned about that, Mr. Channing. I don't know if anyone has explained this to you, but most of the boys there are known as *luqata*—lost, or stray, or fallen things. Like lost property picked up from the ground. In this case, they are abandoned children, foundlings, the products of broken homes. Not orphans in the sense of deceased parents, but children left homeless due to adult misbehavior. Many come from Port Said, where prostitution is rampant because of so many soldiers and sailors passing through. Or they come from families undone by divorce. Normally, a proper orphan is almost always taken in by a relative. But these are boys without acknowledged paternity, who suffer the stigma of illegitimacy and lifelong shame. They often end up on the street, barely surviving by their wits. It's very sad."

"I have noticed how many of them seem angry and depressed . . . I assumed just being in jail would be enough to explain it. But it sounds as though they have suffered a lot more rejection and mistreatment than that."

"It doesn't take them long to understand why nobody wants them," said Miss Finney. "Very hard for them to believe that any adult is on their side. Our chaplains and Bible Women see this often, I am sorry to say."

"If you can arrange your absence at the school, Mr. Channing, you are most welcome to join us on the *Allegheny*. I expect we'll be ready in two or three weeks. Now my friends, let us close our meeting with prayer, and adjourn."

Benjamin took the opportunity to raise the issue of an extended absence with Mr. Fauber, the Director of the Industrial School, asking to meet with him in his office when convenient. Mr. Fauber was always eager to meet with Ben and fill his mind with his pet opinions and theories.

"A journey to the villages sounds most attractive, in many ways," said Fauber. "One can observe the unspoiled native in all his simplicity, where the white man never goes. Away from the turbulence and corrupting influence of the cities. Why, the Egyptian peasant is like a domestic beast in that respect, in nearly a state of innocence."

"It's meant to be a learning experience for me, sir."

"I have no doubt. We shall miss you, however. Your sports activities are proving to be an effective motivator for the boys. Some of them whom I never expected to respond to positive reinforcement have begun to try to earn good conduct points, so that they may gain permission to play ball together. They seem very keen on this flag game you've introduced."

"Is that so, sir?"

"Oh yes indeed. Much to be preferred over coercive or punitive measures. Public reprimand, confinement, diet restricted to bread and water, even caning have all been tried on some of these lads. If they collect enough demerits for their offenses, well, after a while it seems like a small thing to just commit more then, does it not? But withholding a coveted reward, that may sometimes have an impact."

Fauber tended to look up at the ceiling when he waxed philosophical. "The regimentation of sports should be a way of training them in obedience to rules. Consistency, hierarchy, discipline. Conformity to expectations, and so on. A bit surprising that these lads would take to it, considering their past experiences."

"Perhaps it depends on how one plays, sir," Ben replied. "Flag football is a very simple game. There really aren't many rules. Really, we just run around and have fun."

"Indeed?" Fauber seemed unclear on this concept.

"Correct me if I'm wrong, sir, but it seems that their usual days are already regimented to a great degree. They all rise at the same time, wash, get their uniforms on, eat their meals as scheduled. The younger ones have two hours of workshop every day, and four hours of school. The boys of twelve or older have four hours of work, then two hours of school. One hour of group marching or calisthenics. An hour of religious instruction. Chores and bedtime as stipulated. Even the light switches are controlled by guardians. The lavatory stalls have half-doors on them. There are watchers in the dormitories, watchers in the courtyard, everything they do is . . . watched."

"Well yes, of course," Fauber responded. "You have expressed the very nature of the Lancaster model of social conditioning. We must make the students feel exposed to scrutiny at all times—not only by the eyes of the staff, but every student must be a monitor of every other. You see, crimes are naturally committed in privacy and by stealth. But here, everything they do is brought to account, or rendered conspicuous by a kind of pervasive and automatic monitoring. It must be universal, impersonal, impartial. Like the force of gravity. That is what teaches them to modify their behavior."

"But does it, sir? I think you just said that our ball games are a strong motivator. And our games are really a respite from the regimentation. They are mainly just free, and fun."

Fauber gave him an indulgent smile, but it was a cool one. "Mr. Channing, I realize that you have little experience in the field of adolescent criminology, but I can assure you that these principles have been worked out in practice, not only at the original Borstal Institute, but at the London County Council School for Waifs and Strays, the Belgian Reformatory at Ypres, and numerous locations across the Empire. This is modern science. We are instilling the discipline, industry, and punctuality that our students' homes, if they had one, clearly lacked.

"We have our orders to clear this country of the paupers and miscreants who commit crimes, harass visitors, and spread disorder and disease. The boys here have been involved in theft and vandalism, throwing stones at police and foreigners, general delinquency and hooliganism. Obviously, these offenses are the result of too *little* supervision, not too *much*. We have the duty to give them the attention they have never had, in their former lives of vagrancy and neglect. This is our task, Mr. Channing, and we shall achieve it."

"I see . . . thank you, sir."

"Thank you, Mr. Channing. Carry on."

Ben began working with his flag-football club to ensure that they enjoyed even more freedom and spontaneity in their games than before. His club became so popular that he had to divide it into two sections and meet them at the Industrial School twice a week.

Thursday, 1st of March 1923
7:00 a.m.
Danasur

Mother Dear,

How I wish that I could show you where I am right now! I don't think I can describe it adequately in words, though I will do my best.

We are "camping" on a *dahabiya*—a houseboat—on the largest canal streaming north from Tanta. Many thanks to the good people of Allegheny Presbytery who gave the funds to build this boat! Last night we arrived at this mooring and tied up the boat just as the sun was beginning to set. I declare, Mother, if I tried to portray for you the sunset skies, I would never have room to write about anything else.

First, let me explain about the *dahabiya*. It's like a narrow barge, about 60 ft long, with eight sleeping cabins below. Above there is a deck the whole length of the boat, with a center area covered by an awning, where there are simple divans or benches along the sides and a wooden table down the middle. That's where I am right now. I was so excited about being here that I woke very early this morning and could not get back to sleep, so I crept out of my tiny cabin and came up here where there would soon be light enough to write.

It was a chilly morning, just short of frost, with white mist rising from the water. I sat watching the dawn break in a glow of peach, pink, amber and purple; then it turned suddenly to a jonquil yellow, and it was day. There, you see—no sunsets for you, but a sunrise all the same.

How tiny is my cabin? It's a box eight feet long and four feet wide, into which are jammed a bunk and a chair, a washstand, a mirror, a shelf with a little fence around it for toiletries, a row of hooks on the wall, and two drawers under the bunk for clothing. One must travel light on these trips. I cannot stand up fully without my head hitting the ceiling.

My books are stacked on a ledge above the bunk so if there is any rough water they can fall down and clobber me. But the water is normally as smooth and level as a sheet of glass, though with a perceptible current beneath the surface.

As you know, I am not a small man, so the cabin is a bit cramped. There are two slightly larger ones, but one of those is for Mr. and Mrs. Reed, and the other is for their two little children, plus the nanny, a girl of about fourteen. Also with us in small bunkrooms like mine are Doctor Grant and Mikhail Abd al-Massih, a native evangelist from Menufiya who assists Dr. Grant. One of the rooms below is used to store provisions, one as a bath and toilet room, and one as crew quarters, though the men generally prefer to sleep on the deck, for the fresh air I guess. Our rooms have mosquito netting, a blanket, and a mattress and pillow stuffed with what feels like sand.

You may be wondering, why do we itinerate in a houseboat? Well, remember the watery world of the Delta in which we live. Many villages are inaccessible by train or motorcar and can only be reached by long walks or riding upon an animal. In some areas they use what is called the Delta Car, a small wagon-lit that can be attached to a train and then held at a siding during visits. It's important to be able to stop at small towns where we cannot obtain lodging or available food without creating a hardship for those we come to serve.

In the stern, the men are cooking breakfast now in a sort of semi-enclosed galley. I can smell the *fule* or fava beans and it is giving me a great appetite. They stew the beans slowly into a sort of thick paste, then serve it smeared on their rough, round, flat loaves of grayish bread piled high with chopped onions and tomatoes. Also a lot of lime juice and garlic, and I like to put chopped hard-boiled eggs on top as well. That may not sound delicious—especially for breakfast—but I love it. Filling and nourishing, too.

In addition to the aroma of the bubbling *fule* there is a strong scent from the water's edge of bulrushes, flowering beans, and other organic things, but it is not unpleasant. I see a black ox tethered in a field of clover where it is allowed to graze. It's surprisingly noisy here: the braying of donkeys, the incredible moaning of camels, and the barking of dogs. The sunlight has now burned away the mist and the air is as soft and sweet as one can imagine, with just a slight hint of warmth.

Others are coming upstairs now, and the men wish to lay the table for breakfast. Far be it from me to stand in their way! I will continue this narrative later.

Danasur
7:40 p.m.

What a day we have had! It started with a boatside clinic conducted by Doctor Grant and his helper Mikhail. While we were still having breakfast, people began to gather along the edge of the canal and wait. They have a way of crouching down on their haunches that exposes only the soles of their feet to the earth so they don't get dirty. Or perhaps I should say, dirtier.

While they wait, Mikhail speaks quietly to each one, sharing a little Scripture with them and often a word of prayer. Doctor Grant sets up an open-air station on the deck and sees the patients one by one.

I have learned that Doctor Grant is a noted authority on a specific kind of Egyptian iron deficiency anemia. The patients develop a sort of whitened face, eyelids, and tongue . . . it's so pronounced that even I could perceive it. Grant says it is officially anemia if the blood serum ferritin level falls below 25 ng/ml; Grant says he often sees values as low as 15. But it's seldom necessary to do any testing because the symptoms are so evident.

It's not just the pallor, they often feel quite ill as well. The patients were complaining of feeling very tired and weak, often light-headed; some had a buzzing sensation in the ears, "like a beehive" they said, or vertigo. Some showed us brittle nails or loss of hair. And Grant believes that they typically have blood in their stool, but they were averse to discussing this with us. They would use some euphemistic expression, such as "a disturbance in the central provinces" to allude to intestinal troubles.

He says that the anemia is usually caused by a parasitic disease. Specifically, a nematode infestation in the small intestine, which is commonly called hookworm. Logically, there is no point in treating the anemia with iron supplements unless one defeats the parasite first. So Doctor Grant uses a regimen of two treatments of thymol capsules, administered one week apart.

Each patient must swallow the capsules in the presence of the doctor . . . if you give them a second dose to take a week later, they are more than likely to take it at once, on the theory that if one capsule is good, two must be better. So, we plan to return to Danasur in a week's time to treat these patients with their second dose. That requires taking good chart notes to ensure accuracy (that is how Grant used my small amount of help) and writing in India ink on the patient's arm the date and time of treatment.

I hope these details have not disgusted or distressed you. No doubt as the mother of three, and now grandmother, you are fully aware of human physical processes.

I found it all quite fascinating. The basic chemistry and biology I took in college came in handy. It made me wish, however, that I had studied medicine. The contribution of a devoted missionary doctor is second to none.

Doctor Grant also examines patients with other illnesses and refers them if necessary for further treatment, usually at Tanta Hospital. Doctor Hessburgh is their general surgeon, so all patients needing an operation are sent to him, while those with respiratory difficulties (and there are many) go to Doctor Mourad.

Before I continue, let me try to describe our patients. They are farmers, the peasant class which is called here *fellahin*. They were all men, because women find it nearly impossible to subject themselves to the attention of a foreign male physician. Hence the urgent need for female medical missionaries to do this work. The men are nearly all illiterate manual laborers, but that does not mean that they are simple. Many are very intelligent and value learning but have no access to schools except the basic memorization training for young boys at the mosque.

In the Delta, the most elite social class—only about 7% of the population—owns 70% of the productive land, especially in lucrative crops like cotton. The *fellahin* are looked upon as creatures ordained by Allah to produce wealth for their masters. The small portions of land that they control are used for the subsistence of their families and animals.

Imagine them all lined up upon the bank of the canal, wearing a loose cotton shirt and breeches, a *galabiya* or long gown in cotton or wool, a woolen cloak, a skull-cap or small turban wrapped around with a warm shawl, and sandals or bare feet. It's a commonplace observation to say that they could be straight out of the world of the Bible, but it's true.

I assisted Doctor Grant with his clinic until it was time to go into the village for evangelistic work. One must wait until the most urgent daily chores of the farmers are done, which they begin early in the morning. By noon there is a lull in their activity, when they will pray the *zuhr* or noon prayer, eat a meal and have a rest, especially in the summer when the midday heat is burdensome.

We moved in single file along a raised ridge from the canal; there was a ditch of muddy water on one side and a ditch of thick mud soup on the other, with a passage of packed earth about eighteen inches wide between them. Fortunately the little white donkeys are as sure-footed as mountain goats. I have not yet seen one take a step amiss.

It was about thirty minutes' ride through the fields, and they are so lush and beautiful. Magnificently healthy and green, full of small wildlife, especially birds, such as egret and hoopoe, looking exactly like the elegant birds in Pharaonic tomb paintings. The people keep flocks of hens, geese, and ducks, and also we saw many towers for pigeons. These are tall structures made of clay pots lying on their sides, plastered together with mud, where the pigeons can nest safe from predators. Their meat is considered a delicacy (though I have tried it, and to me it seems nearly all bones), and their droppings are valuable as fertilizer. In the evenings, they swoop about in flocks above their towers, until their owners spread grain for them to bring them all home. It's a lovely sight.

We passed pretty orange and fig orchards, and great clusters of the majestic Egyptian palm. These are not like any of the puny ornamental palms you may have seen. They are mighty trees, tall as a flagpole, bursting at the top into graceful long fronds of green. The date harvest has passed but in the fall they are lavish in producing their delicious fruit. Their shade is also highly prized when the sun is at its height.

The village was of course built upon a small rise; all areas subject to the annual inundation of the Nile are sown in crops, with barely a speck of land wasted. The houses of nearly everyone are humble brown shelters of mud brick. But the town has a few prominent structures referred to as "the white ones"—limed, and sometimes painted. We passed the home of a *hadji* who had been on a pilgrimage to Arabia. One outer wall of his house was plastered and painted with scenes of travel—a camel caravan, a train—and the holy enclosure in Mecca where they say their special prayers.

Mr. Reed and Mrs. Reed split up at this point and went door to door inviting people to attend a gathering in the late afternoon, after the *salat al-asr*, or three o'clock prayer. Often we were invited in (I went with Mr. Reed, as Mrs. Reed visited the women), sometimes drank tea, chatted with people, and were hospitably received. Several of those we met had been treated at the Tanta Hospital so they had a positive association with the American Mission already.

That afternoon, we tried to gather at the home of one of the Christians in town, but there were too many interested persons, so we took the men to the spartan little church (just a mud structure with a courtyard where everyone sits on the ground, in the dust) while Mrs. Reed met with the women in the house. Mr. Reed preached upon the text from Isaiah 43, "Fear not, for I have redeemed thee; I have called thee by name, thou art mine." It soon became apparent that perhaps half of the listeners were Muslim, perhaps attracted by the novelty of the occasion. To my surprise, almost all of them stayed for the entire meeting.

Peter Reed had intended, I believe, to speak words of encouragement to those sheep already of the fold; the poor isolated Christians in the Delta experience constant social pressure to turn Mohammedan, and often the aim of evangelism is just to save them from that fate. But he expanded his message to share the good news that the God of the Christians has also redeemed the Muslim listeners and called them lovingly by name as well, and that the promise of salvation and eternal joy also applies to them.

He arranged before we left to gather the Christians together for more intensive discipling on the following day, Friday, during the weekly mosque worship, thinking that the Mohammedans would thus be otherwise occupied.

On our way back to the boat, Mrs. Reed told us that she too had experienced an unexpected complication. She was teaching about the virtues of a Christian home, full of unity and companionship for the family instead of segregation by sex, with mutuality, stability, partnership, and the education of women and girls. But several of the women were Muslims who began to boast that they couldn't read and that they were kept at home by jealous husbands, as evidence of their value. Their fathers and husbands were said to be protecting them like a precious possession. Mrs. Reed it seems took issue with that interpretation.

It was nearly dark when we got back to the boat, yet nobody fell off the narrow footpath into the muddy ditches. We ate a little supper and then retired.

Friday, 2nd of March 1923
4:00 p.m.
Danasur

Dearest Mother,

This has been a troublesome and disappointing day. I considered not telling you about it at all, but I don't think that's fair to you. I will try to summarize it as objectively as possible.

In the morning, I assisted Doctor Grant with his boat clinic, while Peter Reed went into the village ahead of us. He wanted some time to meet with the leaders of the small Christian community for the sake of upbuilding and encouragement, with prayer and Bible study especially for them. They met in the home of one of the village elders. As Mr. Reed told us later, he thought it odd that those attending seemed to be trying to slip in privately without being seen, and some that he was expecting failed to attend at all. They seemed anxious but did not want to tell him what was bothering them.

They have been without consistent Christian support since the native evangelist in Danasur died last year. That may help to explain why their walk of faith seems a bit shaky.

Late in the morning, I accompanied Mrs. Reed to the village. We found that people trying to walk to the church were being stopped by groups of men standing at the street corners, who demanded their names and behaved in an intimidating manner. I'm not sure whether they were even men from the village, or outsiders. Some of the Christians turned around and went home, which is understandable, while others walked with us toward the church, perhaps feeling safer in our company.

When we got to the church, we found a ring of men standing around the entrances, blocking access to the courtyard. With some alarm I noted that several of them were carrying farming implements, such as hoes and spades. Mr. Reed was standing among them, trying to reason with them peaceably. He was telling them that all we wanted was to gather together and pray, just as Muslims do at the mosque, but this seemed to make them more upset.

They accused him—and us—of only pretending to come to their village to help them with medical care and the like. They claimed that these acts of kindness and love are done not for their sake, but for some reason of self-interest known perhaps only to us. They accused us of coming there merely to heap up merit on our own account, to balance some debt of evil-doing or sin so that God will not punish us for it. I heard Peter Reed trying to explain that the free gift of grace cannot be earned through works, but they were having none of that.

At best, they said, we were there only to win them over from Muhammad to Jesus Christ, also perceived to be an interested motive. Our real aim was to denigrate Islam and commit blasphemy—a very serious charge, I assure you. The thing is, I have never heard Peter do that. He is not one of those missionaries who try to attack Muslim belief or practice, or argue the doctrinal superiority of Christianity over Islam. That is an aggressive posture leading only to defensiveness on their part. They can't have got that impression from listening to him.

Then they scolded Mrs. Reed for trying to alienate their wives and daughters and turn them into wanton heathen women. At this point the cluster of women standing to one side all began to cry at once. That in itself was disconcerting. Lydia Reed tried to comfort and soothe them.

Finally, to avoid further conflict, the Christians all gave up and dispersed, and we had no worship service in Danasur today. Rather dejectedly, we followed them, met with them in their homes for a little while to pray and weep a bit, and just to listen to them in their fear and dismay. We came back to the houseboat in the afternoon for a small prayer meeting of our own.

I suppose we can shake the dust from our feet and move on to the next town. But those poor believers must stay there among their hostile neighbors and try to love them, today, tomorrow, and every day after that. Pray for them, Mother, with all your heart.

CHAPTER 6

Tᴴᴇ itineration on the *Allegheny* lasted a full three weeks, and there was not much more of the hostility and intimidation they encountered at Danasur. In the villages where native evangelists were posted, they were received joyfully and with much sacrificial hospitality; people who had barely enough to live on wanted to expend it upon their guests.

Benjamin became attached to Doctor Grant and to the Reeds, including their two sweet young children, and friendly with Mikhail Abd al-Masseh. He promised to come visit Mikhail in Menufiya at his earliest opportunity.

Ben had been back in Tanta for a little more than a week when Peter Reed appeared unexpectedly at Ben's apartment.

"Peter! A welcome surprise. What brings you here?"

"I've just come from Tanta Hospital, where they received this letter hand-delivered from Cairo. It's for you, obviously. I told them I'd bring it right over here."

"If you'll excuse me, I think I'd better have a look," said Ben, opening the sealed letter. "Yes, it's from Mr. Zwemer. That's odd . . . he's inviting me, of all things, to a gala event at the Abdeen Palace. What . . .? It seems there is a charity ball to raise money for organizations serving in Egypt in various ways . . . though what that has to do with me I'm not sure."

"Oh, that's an annual event. A very lavish party. They invite all of Egypt's upper crust and charge them a certain amount to enjoy an evening at the Palace, and the proceeds go to the orphanages, dispensaries, and schools they endow. The money doesn't go to us. We are invited as a form of thanks or recognition for the ministries we carry out in Egypt."

"But why include me? Oh, I see. Zwemer says that there is an important Presbyterian guest coming, a donor from Pittsburgh . . . a lady called

Suzanna Hardy. And she needs an escort for the evening. Listen to this: 'I believe you are the member of the American Mission most familiar with these social circles, and likely to have appropriate attire at hand; formal evening dress is required.' Ouch, that's just a bit barbed, isn't it?" They both laughed.

"We've never been invited to the charity ball. I guess they know the Reeds are not chic enough for that."

"The funny thing is, I *do* have evening wear with me. It's ridiculous how much I packed." Mr. Reed looked at the way Ben was dressed at that moment. He was wearing a crew-necked pullover, knee breeches, stockings and leather football shoes.

"Yes . . . all right, Peter, I did bring football kit. Also my baseball uniform and cleats, and even a pair of indoor basketball shoes, though it doesn't seem likely that I'll need those. Listen, I'm just on my way out the door for football practice at the Borstal. Would you like to come? Get a look at what we're doing over there?"

"Why yes, I've got a few minutes. I'll come with you."

They walked together over to the Industrial School. "As you'll see, the Football Club is more popular than ever. I've divided it into sections by age, and we meet three times a week."

"That's great progress."

"I suppose so, but the alternative is an hour of calisthenics with the guards. Naturally they want to avoid that."

"Granted . . . but at least they don't see you in the same category."

"I'm trying to be something appreciably different. Not a guard, not a teacher. You'll see that they call me 'Coach.' At least to my face . . . who knows what they call me amongst themselves? They call Mr. Fauber '*Al-Awgooz*,' the Old Man."

"The appellation of prison wardens everywhere, I suppose. If they're lucky."

They went through a security check at the gate and had to explain who Mr. Reed was, and permission from Mr. Fauber was sent for. As soon as they entered the courtyard, a crowd of boys aged twelve to fourteen came swarming over to greet them, shouting, "Coach! Coach!" Channing introduced Mr. Reed as a friend of his, and then sent him over to a bench to observe. The boys, of course, were well accustomed to being watched.

Ben opened the two big canvas *shantas* he had brought full of sports equipment, and in a moment they were formed up into teams and playing flag football with limitless energy.

After a while, Ben saw that Mr. Reed had been joined on the bench by Al-Awgooz himself. Fauber began talking Peter's ears off about the modern science of youth reform. Why were certain people so fond of lecturing? Perhaps because they believed they were always right.

In the years following the 1919 uprising and Egypt's mock independence, there was a strengthened movement among the elite to express their nascent nationalism through charitable works. Huda Shaarawi's clinic for women, the Mabarrat Muhammad Ali, secured the patronage of several Turkish princesses and even that of Queen Nazli, the wife of King Fouad.

Some of these associations took on a feminist political aspect as well. Upper-class women like Huda began to call for mandatory and universal education for girls, widely available instruction in homemaking, hygiene, nutrition, and child care, formal training for women in medicine and hospital nursing, and even for greater legal equality in inheritance and divorce.

They argued that a nation is only as free and equal as its women. Huda herself was now a wealthy widow with money from her father and her late husband under her control, and she began to attend congresses of international women's rights organizations in Europe, an experience that left her exhilarated with freedom and charged with determination to help poor women who were still entirely powerless in their families and society.

But the rhetoric of charitable obligation was mixed at the time with the language of colonial repression, to an uncomfortable degree. Fighting crime and social deviance was a top priority of the British occupiers. They poured their resources into prison construction and modernization, the employment and training of police officers, behavioral reform and vocational training for adult convicts.

It was a natural move for them to concentrate on crime prevention as well, which meant getting the reckless youth of Egypt's streets under control. They focused on the youth reformatories at Tanta and Giza, but also on programs for children who were not yet in trouble with law enforcement but simply candidates for juvenile delinquency. Orphanages and training schools for indigent children were meant to clear the streets of a primary nuisance and bring Egypt's cities up to a supposedly civilized Western standard.

The paternalism of the occupiers and the elite fit together neatly in the *malga* movement, shelters funded by philanthropic and religious bodies. Patrons of these institutions were among those invited to the charity ball at Abdeen Palace each year.

On the twelfth of April, shortly after Orthodox Easter, Ben Channing packed his things and took the train up to Cairo. He checked in to stay at the guest quarters in the American Mission building at Ezbekiya. At the appointed hour he presented himself in Mr. Zwemer's office, clad in his bespoke black evening suit with white tie and waistcoat.

He was introduced not to some chunky gray-haired dowager but to a striking and elegant lady of about thirty-five, Mrs. Suzanna Hardy, widow of the Pittsburgh steel producer John Campbell Hardy. She was wearing a silky emerald gown of the latest Parisian fashion.

They contrasted bluntly with the rather Puritan Zwemers in their dark suit and modest black dress. Mrs. Zwemer was constantly nodding and smiling in that anxious way she had, while Mr. Zwemer looked so serious that he seemed almost angry.

The two couples rode in separate carriages to the Abdeen Palace. On the way, Mrs. Hardy managed in a light and charming way to find out all about Ben and the Channing family. Then they moved on to mutual acquaintances; she knew several people in Boston's Beacon Hill area. Eventually they learned that she had met Ben's older brother James in New York City. Ben discovered that Suzanna and her late husband had been major supporters of Presbyterian mission projects for many years, especially Asyut College in Egypt, and Hardy College in Buraan. She was fascinated by Ben's work at the Borstal and asked him many intelligent questions about it.

Their carriage arrived at the extensive gardens of Abdeen and joined the queue to deliver passengers at the grand entrance. It was a mild spring evening, not quite dark yet, but the whole building blazed with light.

"Oh, isn't this fun?" said Suzanna. "Never been inside one of the royal palaces in Egypt before."

"That makes two of us," said Ben.

As people alighted from their carriages, they were joined to another queue, and taken on a long slow tour of the public rooms of the palace, the *salamlek*. It seemed clear that viewing the rooms was regarded as part of the entertainment.

They trooped through the Suez Canal Hall, the Muhammad Ali Hall, the Green, Blue, Red, and White Sitting Rooms, admiring the highly polished parquet floors, the coffered ceilings, baroque detailing and furniture. Marble fireplaces, ormolu clocks, golden candelabras, Sevres vases, classical statues, landscape paintings, several impressive Pharaonic objects.

Then they reached the Throne Room, in an extravagant Islamic style, done up with multicolored rare stone, carved and inlaid wood, stained glass, chandeliers, calligraphy, and all of the ornamentation of a magnificent mosque, yet full of Louis XIV furnishings.

"Gracious," whispered Suzanna to Ben. "It's the spoiled child of Versailles and the Alhambra."

"It would be like living in a museum," Ben replied.

They were led through the greenhouse-like Conservatory, said to be King Fouad's favorite place in the wintertime, and on to the Dining Hall, designed again in a combination of the rococo and arabesque styles. Round tables for ten were set up throughout the great hall, laden with huge floral arrangements, lovely gold-rimmed place settings, crystal goblets and glasses, and silver vessels so frequently polished that they looked almost white.

Each pair of guests gave their names to a liveried attendant and were shown to their places. Ben seated Mrs. Hardy and then took his own seat, across the table from the Zwemers and beside a hefty matron and her heftier husband, in the full dress and decorations of a Colonel in the Dragoon Guards. A high-ranking British government official sat across from them with his wife, and another bureaucratic type, evidently his aide.

Ben glanced around the room at all of the scarlet or blue military tunics, gold braid, and bright medals, civilian formal wear, and many ladies in their best jewels and evening gowns. At one end of the room he saw a high table where King Fouad sat with a few select guests.

At the same time, the veiled Muslim ladies who sponsored charities in the city, such as Huda Shaarawi, were shown to the royal family quarters or *haramlek*, where they were to be hosted by Queen Nazli. Underneath her outer wraps Huda was wearing her best gown and the diamond necklace and earrings given to her as her wedding present or *mahr* by Ali Shaarawi, now many years ago.

Soon the clatter of cutlery and dishes and the murmur of conversation filled the room.

The high-ranking gentleman at their table proved to be Charles Coles, with the title of Pasha; he wore a white satin sash and the medal of the Order of St Michael and St George.

Instinctively everyone allowed him to set the pace of their conversation, and before long Ben learned that Coles Pasha was the colonial Inspector-General for Prisons in Egypt. With him was Mrs. Coles, and the Secretary of the Prisons Department, Papazian Bey.

"Of course, the Nationalists and others very much underestimate our investment in the needy of this country," Coles was saying, as the attendants served a clear golden soup with small soft leaves of basil in it. "We underwrite so many essential social services. Why, building the youth reformatory at Giza cost us over seventy-five thousand pounds. The annual expenditure to run it amounts to another fourteen thousand, if I am not mistaken, Mr. Papazian?"

Papazian Bey quickly replied, "Yes indeed, sir, quite right."

"Seldom does one of these voluntary philanthropic organizations come up with funds like that, to be sure."

"That's a sad fact," agreed Mrs. Watterson, wife of the red-jacketed Colonel. "Why, our charitable fund at the All Saints Cathedral raises only about eleven thousand Egyptian pounds per year. But we like to think that it is very wisely spent."

"Indeed yes," added Mrs. Coles.

"Not everyone would agree, sir, that a youth reformatory is purely philanthropic in nature," Ben ventured to say. "We are intending to help the boys, that is certain. But incarcerating them is also highly coercive. It's fundamentally a law-enforcement effort."

Coles Pasha peered at Ben as if noticing him for the first time.

"The name's Channing, sir. I'm a volunteer at the Industrial School in Tanta."

"Pleased to make your acquaintance, Mr. Channing," Coles said politely.

"I'd say it's obvious that every kind of philanthropy contains an element of social control," Suzanna Hardy said. "As a donor, I've had to accept that fact as the worm in the apple, so to speak. Truly disinterested service is really quite rare."

"Why, what could possibly be wrong with control?" asked Colonel Watterson. "Heaven knows it's hard enough to train any kind of discipline into these people. Only try to command an Egyptian regiment, then you'll see. Or cope with the lot of petty clerks and loafers they give us to staff our offices. These *effendis* are filled with nothing but envy and malice toward

England. It seems they gratify their vanity by not doing anything we expressly desire them to do."

"Not to mention the Egyptian domestics," added Mrs. Watterson. "Such a lot of lie-abouts you never did see."

"They're all just Nationalist agitators. If any man comes before you in a Western suit and a *tarboush*, you can easily assume he is up to no good," Watterson concluded.

Suzanna spoke up again. "I see that King Fouad is wearing a *tarboush*," she said.

All heads swiveled toward the high table, where the King was indeed wearing European formal dress, sashes and medals, and a red felt *fez* with a gold medallion upon it. The sharp points of his waxed moustache made him look somewhat sinister.

"The King is not an Egyptian," Coles pointed out. "He doesn't even speak Arabic. Mainly Italian, I'm told."

"And Queen Nazli speaks French for the most part," said Mrs. Coles. "I have visited the royal harem. There is nothing Egyptian at all about it, as far as I can see."

"That does rather make one aware of what the Nationalists are upset about," said Ben.

"Nonsense, my boy," said Coles. "The Egyptians are a submissive race. They need leadership." At this point the attendants removed their soup plates and replaced them with a dish of salmon and sole *en timbale*.

"If I might direct us back to the subject of philanthropy," interjected Samuel Zwemer, addressing them for the first time. "Disinterested philanthropy, I should say, is indeed possible, and it is the exclusive attribute of the Christian. We understand clearly from Scripture that salvation cannot be earned through good works but is purely the gift of grace. Also, that a sign of the Kingdom of God, and of the redeemed life, is the desire to help and to heal and to serve. I'm afraid this distinction is very difficult for the Muslim mind to grasp."

"Yes, they misinterpret our motives all the time," groused Coles. "The Reformatory boys seem to think that we are there to oppress or exploit them somehow. Yet we are preparing them for a more successful and productive life. We scrape up the dregs from the streets and teach them carpentry, pipe-fitting, metal work, leather crafts, the sewing of canvas bags and other trades. Tonight after dinner you will enjoy a performance by the

Giza Reformatory fife and drum corps, including the bagpipers, taught by a Scots sergeant. Isn't that right, Papazian?"

"Exactly, sir," his assistant confirmed. "There is always a demand for the bands to appear at weddings and festivals, and people are ready to pay three pounds three shillings and expenses for it."

"And of course it gives these boys an honest livelihood upon release. There is even some competition to hire our boys when they leave us, because they have been taught how to work."

"Yet do they respond with gratitude for all that we have done for them?" asked Mrs. Coles. "Our occupation saved Egypt from financial ruin. We created a civilized and efficient army and police, and a court system based upon European ideals. Our engineers made irrigation reliable at last, built proper dams and barrages, designed their roads and railways, postal system, telephones and telegraph. Why, Lord Cromer was indubitably the very father of modern Egypt."

"He was that finest of all possible rulers—a benevolent despot," added Coles.

"And of course, our voluntary and religious organizations created their best schools and hospitals and orphan asylums," said Mrs. Watterson. "These locals here tonight have only imitated the model and example set by us."

The fish was then replaced by a *fricandeau* of veal with braised vegetables.

"Perhaps though, now is the time for them to enjoy the democracy and self-determination we expect for ourselves," Ben said.

"Democracy in this country would only unleash the fury of the militant Islamists," snapped Zwemer, attempting to put Channing in his place. "The Muslim majority would be easily guided by them to create a monstrosity of religious reactionary rule. It would be the end of all possible freedoms, not the dawning of liberty from some dark night of imperialism. You really must stop reading the propaganda in the tawdry Egyptian press."

"I remember at one time suggesting to Lord Cromer that perhaps we should hand over the Reformatories to the educational establishment, rather than the Prison Service," mused Coles, his mind still tracking with the earlier conversation. "His reply was, 'You will spoil the whole show if you do.' And indeed, it seems we have evolved the right method of educating and reforming juvenile criminals. One may judge from the statistics. After release, the boys are kept under parole supervision for two years, and we have found that only fifteen percent are reconvicted during that period. And sixty to seventy percent continue to work at the handicrafts they learned whilst at the Reformatory. Are those figures correct, Papazian?"

"Perfectly, sir."

"The Reformatory boys are also a good source of recruits for the Egyptian Army," Colonel Watterson observed. "They already understand roll call, marching, and drill. We can scoop them right up and sent them to the Sudan."

The next dish offered was a cold breast of duck with tomato aspic and lemon mayonnaise. Offered with it were tiny crisp crackers and another nice wine. Ben and the Zwemers abstained from alcohol, and Suzanna seeing this did so too.

"I must say, however, they would be completely helpless without their English officers," the Colonel continued. "We have Egyptian subalterns of course, but we use them mainly for birching the Sudanese recruits. Muslim to Muslim, you know, creates less offense. But we must at all costs avoid fraternizing with them. Separate messes for the English and Egyptian officers—it's the only way. Clearly, one could not expect British serving officers to eat at the same table with men who belong to the class of tram-conductors and barbers."

"I share a table with my Egyptian colleagues every day," said Ben.

"Ah, but you must picture the military context," said the Colonel. "The young British officer with the height and manly figure that goes well with a smart uniform, well-bred, handsome, fair hair and fair bright coloring. Contrasted with the small and sallow Oriental, it's so eloquent of the high qualities of a martial race. Is it any wonder they have that swagger the natives so resent? The yellow Gyppies hate them for their very distinction and fine manner."

"What a little god is the British officer in Egypt!" murmured Suzanna quietly to Ben.

Benjamin could almost feel the presence of Doctor Mourad sitting beside him at the table. "But surely, sir," he objected. "It's not fair to generalize so broadly about any race or class of people. In my experience, the world is made up of individuals, who may or may not conform to the standards you have stated."

Out of the corner of his eye, Ben could see on Suzanna's lips a subtle smile.

"Your experience, eh? Your vast experience?" chuckled Watterson. "When you've lived here twenty years, my boy, we'll listen to your experience."

"Have all of you been following the wonderful news from the Valley of the Kings?" Suzanna broke in, brightly. "I've only just come from there. Sadly, I arrived just a bit too late to snag a tour of the Tutankhamun tomb. They have already closed it up and reburied it for the season. But dear Lady Evelyn did show me around the magazine, and I must say, the objects they are discovering are nothing short of incredible."

"Lady Evelyn Herbert?" said Mrs. Coles. "Daughter of Lord Carnarvon?"

"Yes, of course. They're not letting anyone else in at the moment. Howard Carter is guarding the tomb like a junkyard dog. But they can't very well keep out the patron of the project, now can they? I've known Eve—Lady Evelyn—for years. We're great friends. We once volunteered together at the Gournia dig on Crete with Harriet Boyd, at the Mycenaean site. In fact, I once considered buying up the concession and sponsoring Carter's Valley of the Kings project myself, but he's done just fine with the patronage of Lord Carnarvon. I'm so happy for them! Five long years of effort and finding nothing. Just last summer, they considered ending the project. And now this!"

"We've been reading about it in the *Times*, of course," said Mrs. Coles, seething with jealousy at the access of this untitled American.

"Well, if you could only see these spectacular things . . . they have just begun unpacking the outer chamber, which was a terrific jumble of large objects, mainly. Wheeled chariots, carved and inlaid beds in the shape of animals, cunning little chairs and other furniture, portable shrines with doll-sized deities inside, heaps of jugs and chests and curious egg-shaped ceramic containers. Heaven knows what's in them. Many of these have been moved to the workroom, where they are photographed and cataloged, and then to the magazine, where they are wrapped and stored. I could see and touch some of them. You'll be able to see them in Cairo soon—they are being boxed up and sent to the Museum."

"Extraordinary," muttered Mrs. Coles.

"And then there were these two amazing life-sized figures, one on either side of the door to the burial chamber. Black, like ebony or pitch, with clothing and crowns of gold-leaf on wood, holding weapons of a sort. Guarding the tomb. So dramatic, it gives one shivers in a way."

"Can't begin to imagine what is inside the burial chamber," said Ben.

"Indeed! You know they did open a little bit of the inner portal, in February. Peeked in just enough to come up against a solid wall of gold, what appears to be a massive gilded shrine. Don't ask me how they ever got such a thing into that enclosed space—I have no idea. The Pharaoh's mummy is likely to be right inside that shrine, untouched since they buried him more than three thousand years ago!"

"A great lot of wretched paganism, if you ask me," said Zwemer, failing to notice that nobody had.

Although Tut's tomb as a topic of conversation did little for Suzanna's present table companions, it had touched off a fever of excitement all over the world. Press attention and public interest were insatiable. Howard Carter was fighting to keep control of the tomb and its contents, while antiquities officials, celebrities and public figures of all sorts, reporters and curious onlookers were turning the Luxor site into a circus.

It was true that they had been searching for this last known missing royal tomb since Carnarvon's excavation permit was granted in 1917. Much of the Valley of the Kings had already been searched down to bedrock. But what made the difference for them was clearing a small triangular area where the earth and rocks dug out by earlier excavations had been dumped, and where small shelters for workers stood, just below the entrance to the tomb of Ramses VI. These things had been there so long that they seemed part of the landscape. But in the 1919–20 season, they set about slowly removing the excavation dump.

It was on the fourth of November in 1922—while Ben Channing was still being treated for pneumonia in the Tanta Hospital—that one of the workmen discovered the top step of a previously unknown staircase leading down into the ground. They cleared the staircase and found it blocked at the bottom by a plastered wall. Carter stopped work, ordered the staircase to be filled in again, and cabled Carnarvon back in England at Highclere Castle to come out to Egypt at once.

When Carnarvon arrived, the staircase was uncovered again, and examination of the plastered wall showed the cartouche of Pharaoh Tutankhamun faintly impressed into the plaster. That was the place! There were indications that a robber had begun to sneak into the tomb in antiquity but was stopped by the authorities. The tomb was sealed up again and evidently had not been tampered with since.

They installed a heavy iron grille over the entrance affixed with four padlocks. Then they began to clear the passage beyond it, which extended for about eight meters, only to stop at another sealed wall. Did that wall conceal another passage? Another staircase? Nothing at all?

Inserting a thin rod, they found a space beyond the wall, and with mounting excitement Carter removed a few stones to look inside. Carter squeezed his head and a candle partly into the hole, and remained that way so long that Carnarvon finally barked, "Well? What do you see?"

Carter famously replied, "I see things . . . marvelous things!"

Marvelous indeed, and these were only the objects in the outer Antechamber, which paled in comparison to the magnificent artifacts discovered later in the inner Burial Chamber. The mummy of the Pharaoh was found inside four boxlike nested shrines, then three heavily decorated anthropomorphic caskets, and finally one closely-fitted coffin of solid gold. But it would take another two years of painstaking work to get to the point at which the king's many sarcophagi could be opened.

Suzanna Hardy went from her exciting visit in Luxor down to Asyut to spend some time at the American Mission College she helped to support. What she did not know, on the night of the gala dinner at Abdeen Palace in Cairo, was that shortly after she left, Lord Carnarvon was taken ill and began to run a fever.

He had been bitten on the face by a mosquito, and then scraped the bite with his razor while shaving. The small wound developed into erysipelas. An unchecked bacterial infection then raged through his body, and on the fifth of April in 1923, Carnarvon died.

His daughter Eve was devastated. She and Carter kept the death quiet as long as they could, in order to notify close family members, but eventually the explosive news was reported, and the world began steaming about the supposed "Mummy's Curse."

It seemed scarcely possible for the Tutankhamun discovery to become even more sensationalized, but it did.

The country's secular nationalists, already upset about so many things, flew into a rage at the way the treasures of Egypt were being appropriated by foreigners. British thieves and adventurers, plundering the wealth and history of their country, which ought to belong to the Egyptians! The archaeologists' claims of scientific motives only masked the pursuit of their own glory at Egypt's expense. It was humiliating.

Emotional objections to the opening of the tomb appeared in the local press. One writer in *Al-Ahram*, the primary Arabic-language daily, addressed the ghost of Tutankhamun directly. "My young king, are they going to transport you to the Museum and set you next to the Qasr an-Nil Barracks, to add insult to injury? So that you might look out upon your occupied country? So that you might see your enslaved people? So that you might learn that those who robbed your grave have dug another for your nation?"

The death of Carnarvon was seen by some as the just recompense for his sacrilege against the ancestors, his usurpation of Egypt's cultural patrimony.

Another source of anger boiled up against the King Tut craze—that of religious nationalists who rejected the identification of the Egyptian people with Pharaonic culture. Hasan al-Banna and his Islamist political movement despised the public's enthusiasm for the customs of a pagan age that had been swept aside by the perfect revelation of Allah. He began writing fierce essays against the revival of the culture of the pre-Islamic past, the time of ignorance, the *jahiliya*. It was just another way for Egypt's enemies to turn her away from Islam.

Doctor Mourad had paid little attention to Tutankhamun's tomb or any other aspect of current events. His life was already busy and complicated enough without having to worry about the fate of some long-dead Pharaoh.

He was hurriedly shopping in the open-air market for fresh fruit and vegetables after work, and planning to run some other errands, when he began to realize that he was being followed.

Four young men, in the typical garb of *effendis*, were shadowing him in the marketplace, gradually approaching. At one fruit stall on the end of a row, they closed in and encircled him.

"O worthy brother," one of them said quietly. "You must grant us a little of your time. We wish to speak with you."

"What's this about?" Mourad replied, his voice rising with alarm. "Who are you?"

"We are friends and colleagues. More than that, your family in the faith."

"I don't know what you're talking about."

"Let us go to a place where we can speak freely. Just over there, we know a place."

They guided him with a little physical pressure to an empty alleyway beside the market.

"Brother, we know that you are a doctor in the hospital of the Crusaders. You work for the Christian missionaries who are corrupting and deceiving our people. These enemies pretend to help the sick, but we know their true aim is to conquer us as the Crusaders of old were unable to do. They seek hegemony over the lands of Islam, hand in hand with their allies the military occupiers. It is a shame, a *shame* that you should be working for them."

"That's rubbish. I help treat patients, that's all."

"Perhaps you think you do, but they are only using you to draw the weak into their nets. They want to destroy Islam and capture all of us as their followers. What they seek is political and cultural domination, and the ruin of Muslim souls."

Other members of the group spoke up. "They desecrate the Noble Quran and slander our Prophet. Every day at your hospital, they blaspheme and defile our faith. They destroy the Egyptian family and lead us into polytheism."

"They undermine our values and make people ashamed of their religion. They educate our girls with false and degrading ideas. Don't you know this? They hypnotize people and turn them against Islam, making them drink wine and eat pork. They compel the sick people in hospitals to pray Christian prayers. They abduct little children and babies and raise them as Christians. They entice older children with pictures and sweets. If the children in their schools and orphanages resist them, they use beating and torture and starvation to force them to convert."

"The people I work with don't do any of those things!" objected Mourad.

"Either you are very naïve, or you are a willing collaborator with them."

"You need to understand! I'm telling you, none of this is true!"

"Doctor Mourad, the four of us compose one cell of a revolutionary organization," said the original speaker. "We want you to join us. Your job will be to supply us with detailed information about what goes on inside the Tanta Hospital. How they try to corrupt the believers and make them Christians. Names, dates, everything. When we have cell meetings, we will let you know, and you will come and make a report. Is that clear?"

"But . . . I . . ."

"Brother, the sacred season of Ramadan will soon be with us. Let it be a time of reflection for you, when you reconsider your errors and find your way to closer obedience."

He did not add—but certainly implied—*we will be watching*.

Mourad gave up his shopping and could not even remember the other errands he had intended to do. He walked home quickly, feeling shaken and afraid.

CHAPTER 7

NEVER before had Doctor Mourad viewed the coming of Ramadan as a threat . . . but now he did.

For one month during the Islamic lunar year, Muslims are expected to abstain completely from all food and drink throughout the daylight hours. The regime is difficult, especially during the long, hot days of summer.

But in the evenings, breaking the fast can be festive and blessed. When people hear the sound of the call to prayer marking the day's end, they often drink water and eat a few dates for a little energy boost, perform the evening prayer, and then sit down to an ample meal with their family and friends.

There is special merit in giving generously to the poor during Ramadan in the form of an *iftar* meal, so even the destitute can expect to eat well at a public table when the sun goes down.

Mourad, however, could be somewhat lax in his fasting observance, for the same reason that he did not always perform every prayer during the day—because he was a working physician who was always busy examining and treating patients, often in urgent situations. He had to keep moving all day and was not able to save his strength or take long naps as some did to get through those hours of hunger and thirst.

But now, he felt sure that his Islamic observance was subject to scrutiny by unfriendly forces. He was under suspicion, an accused collaborator with the Crusaders.

He told himself that those people had no right to judge him. But judge him they would, and he was uneasy about the consequences.

He was sitting with Ben Channing at another outdoor café a few days before Ramadan was due to begin. He hunched over his coffee, feeling conspicuous. Would this look bad, to be hobnobbing with the enemy in the open like this? Or would it be seen as part of his intelligence-gathering assignment?

There were some other men at a table nearby who might have been watching him. But was it only his anxious imagination?

Ben was telling Mourad a long story about something that happened at the Borstal. "That's another one of Fauber's theories, you know, that schools and churches are becoming soft and weak due to too much feminine influence. He says we need to emphasize competitive sports and physical education to further the ideal of Christian manliness. Athleticism as the antidote to flabby modern life, or something. I guess that's where I come in, teaching team sports at the Borstal. According to him, men and boys need a heroic and aggressive Christianity. Then he told me all about some Anglican bishop in India who killed a cobra with a golf club!"

Ben saw Mourad's lack of attention to his words, and watched contradictory feelings passing over his face like clouds.

"Mourad," he said gently, "is something bothering you? You seem preoccupied."

"I'm sorry, Ben. I've had a lot on my mind lately."

"Well listen, maybe you need a diversion. Some of the fellows from my flat are planning to go out Tuesday night. Wissa Buktur and Abbas Bahri, and maybe some others. They say that the custom here in Tanta is to go down to the Badawi mosque on the first night of Ramadan for a sort of little street fair. A morale booster for the fasting season, I gather. Why don't you come with us? Sounds like just a bit of innocent family fun."

"Yes, that's the custom. It's like a little *mulid* or saint's day celebration."

"We're going to meet at the mosque after *iftar*. Come and join us."

Could anyone object to Mourad's presence with Channing at the Badawi mosque? Perhaps he could say that he is introducing this foreigner to the true faith of Islam. Again Mourad scolded himself for second-guessing everything now. He agreed to go with Channing to the Badawi mosque on Ramadan's first night.

The historic mosque—Tanta's claim to fame—stood in the center of the mostly rebuilt old Islamic district, ringed by eight or nine tombs and several shrines in honor of the saint's prominent followers. Al-Badawi was said to have been born in Morocco and migrated to Mecca and Baghdad, where he studied the lore of the Sufi mystics and was initiated into their society. In the year 1236 he settled in Tanta, and became well known for his wisdom and spiritual strength, accumulating an assembly of followers who became the nucleus of the Ahmadiya order of Sufis.

His *mulid* in October developed into one of the great pilgrimage events of the Muslim world, after the *hadj* in Mecca. It attracted thousands of devout worshippers, coming to venerate the tomb of the sheikh and to seek a blessing. There was a wide open space beyond the train station where rows of tents were set up for the pilgrims at the major *mulid*. But this gathering was just a small occasion for local people.

Ben walked down to the Badawi mosque with his flat-mates well after dark on April seventeenth. The young men were all constantly joking and teasing each other.

"You call this a fast?" said Wissa. "One little month? The Copts are the champions of all fasting. We fast for over 200 days a year!"

"It's not the same, Wissa. You don't go without eating for all that time. You just avoid animal products during the fasts."

"Not true, there are abstinent days, like Great Friday and the Nativity. And weeks without all the wonderful foods! Meat, fish, milk, eggs, all of it! Not so much as a chicken soup! The monks in the monasteries eat nothing but black bread that's as hard as a rock. They have to soak it in water just to chew it. Why would a loving God want us to live like that?"

"We can't afford meat anyway," someone grumbled. "Too many cabbages."

"I wonder the same thing about not drinking water during the days in Ramadan," said Benjamin. "We know that dehydration is unhealthy. Makes me wonder whether somebody got Allah's message wrong about how to fast."

"*Ya Binyameen!* Do not let anyone hear you say that! It's blasphemy, my friend."

"Christians in the West are fasting as well, I think? In the weeks before Easter?" asked Abbas.

"Catholics eat fish on Fridays. And some people give up eggs and dairy foods, I believe. But Presbyterians don't really go in for that kind of thing."

"Because you want to be able to have your bacon and your beer, yes?"

"Abbas, you know I don't drink alcohol."

"Well, I can tell you this. Egyptians eat more meat and sugar during Ramadan than all the rest of the year. It's one long party, every night! It's great, as long as you're nocturnal! Not so great if you have to work all day."

They had entered the precincts of the Badawi complex when Doctor Mourad joined them.

"*Inta menawar!*" said Abbas to him. You bring us light!

"*Allah yenawar, ya bey*," he replied.

There wasn't much chatting the rest of the time, because of the loud drumming and music everywhere. Above the mosque's wide forecourt dangled bright strings of brass lanterns or *fanawees*, lighted candles shining within filigree and panels of stained glass. The walls were hung with big colorful banners of the Sufi orders and large framed portraits of their sheikhs. There were several ensembles of frame drums and tambourines, finger cymbals, oddly nasal wind instruments, a shrill drone of strings, and the beautiful Egyptian *oud* or lute, plus many singers, not quite far enough apart to prevent an effect of cheerful but confusing din.

A cadre of stout older women, all wrapped in black, sang together at the top of their voices and clapped their hands to the beat of the music.

Closely-packed crowds moved slowly among the market stalls, where people were selling nougat and other sweets, roasted chickpeas, toys, sugar dolls, party hats, candles, crispy pretzels with sesame seeds, sweet potatoes grilled over hot coals. There were many religious articles for sale: prayer beads, framed calligraphy, sticks of incense, books.

Ben was surprised to see so many young children out and about, thinking it might be past their bedtime . . . but apparently their days were also topsy-turvy during the Ramadan season. At one point he spotted the Reed family at the fair with their two children and the nanny. He could not get close enough to say hello before they disappeared.

The main attraction for the children was all of the special fun going on. There were little metal swing sets and a carousel for kids to ride, acrobats and stunt shows, puppet theaters, and stalls for throwing rag balls at targets like the midway games at the State Fair back home.

"This all seems a bit frivolous for the fasting season," Ben shouted into Mourad's ear.

"Prayer and fasting, food and fun," replied Mourad. "An hour for your Lord and an hour for your heart. Ours is a tolerant and humane religion."

Ben enjoyed it. It was all very *shaabi*, of the people, working class. Maybe sometimes a bit lowbrow, but sincere and full of life.

"You must buy some chickpeas," one of his friends said to Ben. "You don't want it said of you, 'He left the *mulid* with no chickpeas.'"

"What?" said Ben, straining to hear.

"Never mind, I'll explain it later," he replied, laughing.

There was a whole row of charm-sellers, men who would write a specific sacred verse or formula on a slip of paper and enclose it in a little capsule to be attached to one's house, farm animal, child, or self. Charms for fertility and potency were especially popular and benefited from the reputed power of Al-Badawi to convey such a blessing. Many women, themselves illiterate, clustered around these tables.

On the edge of the crowd, they came upon a tattoo booth where a practitioner was applying small images of a bird or a sword or a crescent moon on a man's skin, or a word in Arabic script. Wissa Buktur said to Ben, "Step right up, my friend—you need one of these," pushing up his shirt sleeve to show him a bluish Coptic cross on Wissa's wrist, directly over the blood vessels of the arm. "Every Christian needs this," said Wissa, "so they can't make you change your faith without cutting off your hand."

"And likely bleeding to death," said Ben.

"That too," Wissa agreed.

Just in front of the mosque, a large group of men performed an informal *dhikr* or remembrance of God, to repetitive music. Each man slowly made a half-turn to one side, then a half-turn the other way, again and again . . . left . . . right . . . left . . . right. Arms swinging, hands raised, eyes closed, moving with the rhythm of the chanting. At certain pauses in the music, they all breathed out, "Allah!" It seemed disrespectful to call it a trance, but there was something of a mystical state about it. Ben saw a man cup his hands as if to receive a *baraka* or blessing from above, and then stroke his palms over his face and clothes, spreading the blessing upon himself.

There was a break in the chanting, as everyone took a breather. Then a young man climbed up on the platform to address the crowd.

"Brothers, may the *baraka* of the beloved friend of Allah, Al-Sayyid Al-Badawi, come down upon you," he said. "The exalted Al-Badawi, who fought the French Crusaders here in Lower Egypt, who helped us defeat them at the Battle of Mansoura. At the saint's great *mulid* in the fall, why is there a procession of mock captives wearing Crusader's armor? Because the knights of the arrogant King Louis were taken on that day, and Louis himself was seized and held to ransom. Remember this, my brothers, and picture it in your minds—the King of France in chains, held by the faithful!"

The crowd quieted further in order to hear him speak.

"Yet here in our own city, O Muslims, we have a great Christian school dedicated to the infidel invader, King Louis. How can such a thing be permitted? The missionaries, they fill the minds of our children with falsehoods, they defame the holy religion of Islam, they draw the weak into their own unbelief, where they bear no fruit in this life, and in the Hereafter, they will abide in the Fire! And we allow this wickedness to happen!

"These new Crusaders, they spend their great wealth to hinder our people in the path of Allah. They use their money to make their hospitals, schools, and orphanages, where they lead our people astray. They deceive the poor and needy through these institutions. They make use of the poverty and illness of the people to draw us away from Islam!"

Ben Channing and his friends were on the outer edge of the crowd, but they could hear what the speaker was saying. And Mourad quickly realized that the young man speaking was the same one who had led the group that cornered him in the market square. His mind began to race with anxiety about what might happen next, and how he could move Ben and his group out of the crowded courtyard and away from this place.

The other members of the speaker's cell began to move through the crowd with offering boxes, collecting money.

"How do we eradicate this evil? My brothers, we must establish similar hospitals, schools, and orphanages, to safeguard the poor and the innocent from capture at the hands of the infidels! That requires much giving, O Muslims, to counter their charities with our own. For the Noble Quran teaches, 'Spend of your substance in the cause of Allah, and let not your own hands contribute to your destruction.' And again, in the Surah *al-Baqarah*, 'Whatever you spend in the cause of Allah shall be repaid unto you.' And in the Surah *al-Talaq*, 'Let a man spend according to what Allah has given him.' For the unbelievers have their wealth and they will continue to use it to do evil, but in the end they shall have sighs and regrets; at length they will be overcome!"

Mourad and Abbas, who also understood what was happening, began to press their group gradually out of the crowd. Though it seemed that these men intended to do nothing more than collect money, no one could predict the reaction of a crowd incensed or inspired by religious emotion.

As Ben grasped the situation, he intently scanned the lanes and market stalls for the Reed family, finally spotting them near the children's area. "Mourad, I can't leave yet, I've got to let Peter know," he said.

"Yes, let's move in that direction," Mourad replied.

When they reached the family, they advised them to leave the fair at once and go home. They accompanied the Reeds as far as their gate, then went on past the Municipal Gardens to their flat on Muhammad Pasha Said Street. Benjamin never did get his bag of *mulid* chickpeas that night.

By the middle of May, the heavy heat of summer was fully in command of their lives. Ben Channing had never experienced such heat. It was a relentless force that everyone had to plan their lives around, right down to which side of the street you chose to walk on, where there might be a little more shade.

The full meeting of the Delta Evangelistic Committee took place on the fourth and fifth of June, in the town of Qalyoub. At that gathering, Ben learned that his friend Mikhail Abd al-Masseh was to be moved from Menufiya to become the native evangelist in the town of Danasur. It was unusual for them to post one evangelist by himself in a rural setting, but that village was being neglected, and Doctor Grant agreed that his clinic and the church in Menufiya could manage without him.

Mikhail immediately packed up his few belongings and moved to Danasur. He began visiting every Christian family in the village; on Friday he conducted the first public worship service in their humble church. He was looking forward to the first Sunday with his new congregation.

Also in early June, a British mounted infantry battalion was on maneuvers, moving from Cairo north to Alexandria. They reached a military camp at Khamshish and were ordered to remain there for several days. Unfortunately, there was nothing at all for them do at Khamshish, and they quickly became overheated, bored, and a bit rowdy.

On Sunday the tenth of June, they had a day of rest and slept in well into the morning. A small group of six officers packed their shotguns and a picnic lunch and set off to look for some shooting.

They rode for an hour or so, seeing nothing that looked like interesting game, until they approached the village of Danasur. They spotted some flocks of pigeons circling over the fields on the outskirts of the town, above the threshing floors. There were few people around in the hottest part of the day, since everyone knows that only mad dogs and Englishmen go forth in the noonday sun. They came upon an elderly toothless fellow sleeping in the shade at the threshing floors, who was unable to understand the gestures by which they thought they could secure permission for a shoot. Terrified at the sight of six officers with guns, the old man shuffled away as quickly as he could.

They sat themselves down in the shade of the palms inside the threshing enclosure and ate some cheese and pickle sandwiches, washing them down with a lot of warm beer, resting comfortably on the heaps of soft chaff along the walls. Then they decided to use those walls as a blind from which to shoot at the pigeons still flickering about overhead.

A certain Lieutenant Parker was the first to begin shooting and brought down a few of the pigeons. That got them excited, and in their excitement they failed to notice that the hot brass shell casings ejected from their shotguns had begun to smolder amidst the chaff on the threshing floor. The pigeons, alarmed, moved closer to the safety of their cotes within the village, but each blast frightened them so much that they flew up again in a panic. A plume of black smoke rose from the threshing floor, visible in the village.

At about that time, a delegation of angry people from Danasur arrived, alerted by the toothless old man. They saw Lieutenant Parker fire his gun again at their pigeons. They confronted the six officers, outnumbering them by a factor of ten, and one man—the owner of that threshing floor—grappled with Parker for his gun. In the struggle, the gun went off, and a woman in the crowd dropped to the ground.

The anger of the crowd redoubled, especially when they discovered that the woman was the owner's wife. She was stunned enough by the blast to make them all believe she was dead. In a fury they set upon the British officers with farming tools and the long wooden cudgel called *nabbout*, a weapon so ancient it was pictured in the paintings of Pharaonic tombs.

One soldier, a Captain Bright, was battered in the head, and the ranking officer, a Major Coffen, ordered him to flee with another officer and get help from the base encampment. The other four officers were disarmed, tied up, and held captive. In the melee, Major Coffen suffered a broken arm and another officer a crushed nose, which bled copiously all over his khaki uniform. The people also took possession of the six horses.

By this time, most of the village had been roused from their peaceful afternoon and were told that an army of Christian invaders was coming to destroy their town. Defenders were called forth with whatever weapons they could find at hand. Most of them rushed out to the threshing floors to confront the apparent threat.

But a small contingent turned in another direction: toward the little village church. They found Mikhail Abd al-Masseh with just a few people in the building, having a personal conversation after Sunday worship. Seeing these Christians as infidels colluding with the British occupiers, they attacked them with their hoes and cudgels. Mikhail was beaten with the force of righteous anger. They continued to beat him until he was clearly dead.

In the meantime, Captain Bright and the other officer struggled to run back to the encampment, four miles away. About halfway there, Bright stumbled and fell, and lay unconscious in the searing heat. The other officer pushed on, desperate to reach their base.

When at last he got there, a whole company mounted up and rushed toward the village. On the way they found Captain Bright's body. A man passing by on his donkey had seen the soldier in trouble and stopped to help him, bringing him water from the canal. The soldiers mistakenly thought that the man had killed Bright and promptly shot him.

At the village, they recovered the four captive officers and began arresting men at random.

Perhaps the most remarkable thing about the Danasur incident was the speed with which news of it travelled all over the country, to every city and town, out to the remotest village, through the expatriate and minority communities, and up the chain of command to the British High Commissioner for Egypt, Lord Mosby.

Lord Mosby immediately ordered a special tribunal to try the case under a military decree from 1895, intended to deal swiftly and summarily with any attacks on British soldiers or sailors. Such a tribunal operated outside the normal procedures and protections of the Egyptian colonial courts, possessed the power to inflict more drastic sentences, and prohibited any appeal.

Word also spread quickly up to the Houses of Parliament and the British Foreign Secretary, Sir Edward Grey. Fierce demands for exemplary punishment of the rebellious villagers were heard in government and the London press.

By the fourteenth of June—only a few days after the incident in Danasur—the tribunal assembled at the regional courthouse in Tanta to try the case. The tribunal comprised three British judicial advocates, one Egyptian judge from the Native Courts, and the Minister of Justice.

The Minister who presided over the tribunal, Boutros Ghobrial, was unfortunately a Copt. This fact was taken by many as evidence that Egyptian Christians were indeed traitors to the nation and collaborators with the British imperialists.

Fifty men from Danasur were held in the courtroom in an iron cage, while incomprehensible proceedings took place in English in front of them. In the village, wooden gallows had already been erected.

The men were charged with murder and assault in a "shooting affray," and accused of being part of a pre-arranged conspiracy to attack British officers, probably due to religious or political motives. The prosecution claimed that they had killed Captain Bright and wounded two other officers, who were inoffensively hunting wild birds at the time. They claimed that the officers had received permission to hunt there. They claimed that they were 500 yards from the village and 100 yards from the threshing floors. They claimed that the village men had ambushed them without warning, with the intention of harming them and stealing their horses and weapons. They claimed that the soldiers were acting only in self-defense.

Never in the course of the trial did they hear witness testimony refuting these claims. Nor did they ever explain that the Medical Examiner had determined, upon a post-mortem of Captain Bright's body, that the officer had suffered concussion and sunstroke and thereupon died of "apoplexy." A charge even of manslaughter should have been difficult to sustain.

They also never troubled to establish why, if this were a case of premeditated insurrection and homicide, the people of the village disarmed four of the officers and held them at the scene instead of killing them.

The defense lasted exactly thirty minutes, during which they heard the testimony of a single policeman who arrived at the scene once the incident was over and had no direct knowledge of it. None of the village residents were permitted to testify in their own behalf.

The hearing was soon completed, only one week from the date of the incident; no court proceeding had ever moved so quickly. Four men were sentenced to be hanged, and two to penal servitude for life. Ten more defendants got sentences in prison of up to fifteen years. And eight more were ordered to be flogged. It was stipulated that the sentences of hanging and flogging should be carried out in the presence of everyone in the village—as an example to the others.

On the very next day, the four men are led one by one to the wooden gallows that had already been constructed in the center of Danasur.

Women weeping on the rooftops moan in terror as each man is brought out and his sentence of death read aloud. The women stretch out their arms toward the doomed man.

His hands and feet are bound, and a black hood is placed over his head. Then the noose is fitted around his neck. The assistant stands aside, the hangman shifts a lever, the platform snaps open, and the body drops heavily into space, bouncing up again when its weight comes to the end of the rope. He swings for a moment or two, then he is lowered to the ground, and the next man is readied for his brief moment in history.

For some inscrutable British reason this ritual is carried out at high noon, when the sun is blistering hot. Ranks of soldiers in full uniform stand at attention throughout the event, their buttons and helmets and bayonets blazing in the sun. They seem to derive a perverse pleasure from scrupulously observing ceremony.

In the next act of this drama, the eight villagers to be flogged are brought out together, stripped to the waist, and doubled over wooden sawhorses. Their arms are bound to the crosspieces and their necks held in iron collars. Eight men—brought from the Cairo prison system to this village where they are not known—arm themselves with the *kourbash* or leather whip, and in rhythm to the sound of counting aloud, they slash the sharp bands of the whips against the skin of their victims. Blood spatters, women shriek, the victims howl in pain, men watch with their eyes fixed on the violence and their faces rigid with grief.

Which four men did they hang, of all of those present in the village on the day of the incident? Which ones did they flog? Apparently, it scarcely mattered . . . since none of those men were guiltier than any others. The only persons who actually did commit murder that day, in the deliberate killings of Mikhail Abd al-Masseh and the man who tried to help Captain Bright, were never apprehended, tried, or punished.

They were sitting in the shady garden of the All Saints Cathedral in Cairo, sipping lemonade between sessions. Ben Channing just happened to be there during and after the Danasur tribunal, attending a joint summer conference of the Student Volunteer Movement missionaries and the Young Men's Christian Association in Egypt. He was hoping to pick up some useful ideas about conducting a sports ministry for boys.

"You realize, of course, that all of this will only make our jobs much harder," remarked a young man called Micks.

"I don't see why it should," said another, called Percival. "It's meant to function as a deterrent. Swift justice, firm punishment. Necessary to restore order."

"But it's doing exactly the opposite," said a young lieutenant in the Army of Occupation, a military chaplain associated with the S.V.M. "It actually undermines our authority in Egypt. Makes us look like a lot of vindictive monsters. Of course people are extremely upset."

"They're more than upset," said Ben. "They're furious, devastated, grieved. Don't you pay attention to the Egyptian press? Danasur was an act of vengeance, not justice. It's going to be potent fuel for the Nationalist cause. People all over the country, at every social level, are pouring forth sympathy for the village and disgust at the way they were treated."

"It's unworthy of the traditions of the British Empire," Micks grumbled.

"I don't understand you," Percival objected. "In terms of stability and progress, Egypt is incomparably stronger than when we first took her in hand. The country has advanced many degrees on the scale of civilization, anyone can see that. Lord Mosby has acknowledged that the sentences were severe, but necessary. The behavior of the villagers was unacceptable and had to be curtailed by whatever means lay at our disposal."

"I'm sorry, Percy, I can't agree," said the young chaplain, whose name was Ashdown. "We take credit for Egypt's advances in the area of justice and law, and then we undermine all of that by a ruling in direct contradiction to them. Our claims to a just and enlightened rule have been undone. You must know that hanging and flogging were supposedly prohibited by the colonial government. Yet here we are making use of those measures. We've turned the clock back to the bad old days of Ottoman rule before we arrived."

"Do you know that the sentences were imposed in the name of King Fouad? The King is in Europe—he wasn't even consulted. He had nothing to do with this. Speaks of a rather guilty conscience, don't you think?"

"All of you are missing the essential point," asserted Percival. "Let us recognize the real reason for the uprising of the villagers. The Muslim and his fanatical hatred of all Christians, so passionate as to make him forget all of the benefits that the British have brought to him."

"If they didn't hate us before, they most assuredly do now," said Micks in a gloomy voice.

"All Egyptians are outraged by this incident, not only the Muslims, not only the Nationalists," said Ben. "The simplest farmer in any village sees clearly that he can expect no justice and no mercy from the powerful forces that control his country. It's a moment of collective mourning, a symbol of Egypt's weakness and suffering. I believe it will bring people together in opposition as nothing else could do."

"It's a complete strategic blunder, if nothing else. Even Sir Edward Grey, the Foreign Minister, has said that it discredits the occupation."

"Of course, Grey and the whole government in London are under pressure from Parliament and the public. Grey has actually said that the whole edifice of the worldwide Empire cannot stand if dubious acts by its officials are criticized and its misdeeds denounced due to sentimental interference at home," added Ashdown. "A shocking admission, I must say."

"You know, some of our S.V.M. leaders at home believe that we have a great advantage in evangelism here, where the imperial structure protects us. Well, it also means that we take the blame for their offenses and mistakes."

"And not only you," observed Ben Channing, the sole American in the group. "That applies to all of us."

The meeting reconvened and the participants went back inside.

Laurence Ashdown, the Army chaplain, needed to go from the S.V.M. and Y.M.C.A. conference at the Cathedral to his job on the night shift down in the Fishmarket.

Beyond the Ezbekiya Gardens, off in the direction of the Midan al-Khaznadar and the downscale Hotel Bristol, lay the part of Cairo called the Fishmarket, even though no seafood was sold there. The respectable elements of the Cairo expatriate community knew it by reputation as an infamous den of vice. But for the British Army members of "other ranks," it was their entertainment district.

The Fishmarket was the place to find the dance halls, brothels, gambling tables, and above all the bars, where a man and his mates might find relief from the routine and the vexations of Army life in Egypt.

For Lieutenant Ashdown, it was a constant challenge to somehow keep the soldiers from getting themselves into mountains of trouble through their own heedless behavior.

Nearly every night there was some friction going on, between a soldier and a man he said had tried to rob him, a man who claimed a soldier owed him money, a couple of soldiers sparring over the same woman, and problems of that sort. But lately, since the Danasur story broke, Ashdown had perceived a sharp increase in the seriousness of altercations in the Fishmarket. Often, he had to intervene, and a couple of times he had been forced to call the military police.

He came to one of their favorite haunts, a bar for the heavy drinkers, run by a Greek everyone called "Tony." Ashdown noticed an Army Ford outside parked so clumsily that it blocked the street. In the lighted windows of several apartments overlooking the street stood barely-dressed women in provocative poses, trying to get the soldiers to come upstairs. Loud music and voices came from Tony's open doorways.

It was hotter than an oven inside the bar, full of sweating Englishmen. One group was especially loud and raucous, and Ashdown found a member of the group already passed out from drink. He and another soldier dragged the fellow outside, hoping the cooler air would revive him, and laid him out in the open back seat of the Ford.

Ashdown went back inside to keep an eye on the rest of them. He encountered a young man, less drunk than the rest, in a state of melancholy self-examination, ready to have a talk with a chaplain. They discussed the young soldier's aimless life.

Then Ashdown heard a strange noise from outside in the street: the clamor of a crowd cheering. He was seized by a sudden qualm. Rushing outside, he found the little open Ford engulfed in flames, with the drunken young soldier still in the back seat. From the women in the windows upstairs and passers-by on the street came the sound of a harsh and heartless jubilation.

The chaplain spurred himself toward the car to try to rescue the soldier somehow, but just at that instant, the fire ignited the vehicle's petrol tank, touching off an explosion.

Ashdown was thrown off his feet and into the air, coming down hard on his back, the breath knocked out of him.

By that time other soldiers had started coming forth from the bars and brothels along Rouet Street, and fistfights were breaking out everywhere. Someone discovered Lieutenant Ashdown lying dazed on the pavement and decided to get him to a hospital.

It was the nineteenth of June in 1923. The Feast of Saint Michael the Archangel; the twelfth day of the month of Paona, according to the ancient Coptic calendar. The traditional start to the rising of the Nile. The season of the inundation.

CHAPTER 8

THE traditional date for the peak of the Nile inundation was the Feast of the Holy Cross or Youm as-Salib, a three-day observance at the end of September. It was the ancient Coptic month of Thout. The river was so high then that it served almost as a vacation month for farmers, since no cultivation work could be done with the water covering their fields.

It was a time to plan festivals and weddings, to give thanks for the annual life-giving bounty of the flood, and to be grateful that the hottest part of the year was over.

But in 1923, it was also a time of tension and of violence.

There were numerous attacks on British civilians—beatings, snipers, knives—especially in the Boulaq and Shubra neighborhoods of Cairo, where many civil servants and their families lived. British soldiers in uniform were ordered to avoid moving around the city alone.

Officials of the Egyptian State Railway received threatening letters, and some were shot at. Trains full of passengers were easy targets, especially in Upper Egypt, where assailants could hide in the tall thick sugar-cane and wait for a train to pass by, attack it, and disappear again into the fields.

A simple method of assassination was devised, in which a certain official was stalked on the street, then shot in the back with a handgun. The Commandant of the Cairo City Police, Mr. Thomas Russell, was successfully dispatched in just this fashion. A nationalist cell known as the Inayat Brothers claimed responsibility for his murder.

Rumors circulated of other shadowy organizations offering bounties for the killing of British residents: one hundred pounds for officers or administrators, fifty for British soldiers, twenty-five for civilians, women, or children.

Then, a homemade bomb containing a small vial of picric acid and a charge of gunpowder became a favorite method of frightening people, though it was so unstable that it had limited usefulness as a weapon. But in one lucky attack, the Controller General of the Education Ministry, Mr. Aldred Brown, was killed and his entire family wounded when someone tossed one of these explosives into their carriage.

This outrage led to a mass indignation meeting of British expatriates at Shepheard's Hotel. They demanded better protection from the colonial authorities and crushing punishment for those responsible for these attacks. Lord Mosby was a very sick man at this point, dying slowly from some terrible inflammation of the bowels, unable to take any solid food, surviving on Benger's baby formula, confined to his bed. The many people in Egypt who hated him might have been gratified to witness his agonizing decline.

The powerful imperial machine was faltering.

Yet the daily work went on, including Ben Channing's service at the Industrial School. He found that the novelty of flag football had worn off a bit, and thought that perhaps the boys needed a new challenge. So he decided that it was time for them to learn to play baseball.

"Baseball? I mean, there is no tradition of that game here, at all," Mourad told him. "I gather that the British play cricket and something called 'rounders' at their sporting clubs. I believe they are similar, with batting and pitching and running from place to place. But American baseball?"

"Well, that's the beauty of it, see? It's *not* a British game. It's something entirely new. I'm thinking they will like that idea."

"Perhaps . . ."

"And baseball is the perfect blend of individual performance and team coordination. Each man has to play his own position well, and then the whole group succeeds. I'm seeing that as a kind of object lesson."

"Speaking of objects, where are you going to get enough equipment? Doesn't it require all sorts of paraphernalia?"

"Oh, you don't need that much for a simple sandlot game like I'm planning. And Mourad, you will probably jump on me again if I tell you that I brought a lot of the essential things with me. I also got Fauber's permission to have the shop classes make stuff for us: the leather-craft class is working on mitts, and the woodshop is making bats to match one that I gave them. Even the tailor shop is making some bases out of striped canvas—very colorful. It's working up a bit of anticipation among the boys as well."

"Another thing. What about space? Don't you need a big open field or something like that?"

"There's an unused lot across the street and behind the girls' school that is plenty big enough. It's American Mission property. I went and cajoled Miss Bostram into letting us use it a couple of times a week. No grass, of course, but we can play on packed earth."

"My goodness, you've thought of everything, I guess."

"Probably not. But we'll have enough to get started. We're already working on basic skills—throwing, batting, catching, tagging, learning the rules. I've even got a couple of bigger boys who might coach up to be pretty good at it. There's one in particular . . . his name's Gamahl. I had to convince Fauber to let me work with him, because his behavior isn't that great. Tends to smack the younger boys if they bother him, doesn't do his lessons in the school hours. He hasn't really earned the right to participate."

"That could be a problem."

"But I told Fauber that maybe this would help Gamahl. Give him something to excel at. Some positive attention for a change. If he enjoys it, it might make him want to cooperate."

"Ever the optimist . . ."

"If you're working with troubled kids, you'd better be."

Channing started to wear his Yale baseball uniform to work, on the days when there was team practice. It had his name on the back and a big number 12. The word YALE was written in huge block letters across the chest. His cap was white with a blue bill and a blue letter Y on the front. The boys teased him about the cap, but he could tell they secretly admired it. He got the tailor shop working on some canvas caps to be awarded to the boys who worked hard enough on their skills to make the starting lineup.

An old-fashioned Presbyterian tradition that he could not give up was keeping the Sabbath. Channing declined to work on Sundays. He ended up going to the Protestant church in Tanta on Fridays with his friend Wissa Buktur, and then again on Sundays alone. That meant he heard the same sermon and readings twice, but he found that this was actually helpful for his Arabic learning and that he understood nearly everything the second time through.

One Sunday in October, he noticed a group of visitors he had not seen before. About a dozen young men. And with them, to Channing's great surprise, was a young Western woman.

As soon as he spotted her, he stopped listening to the service. Suddenly there was nothing else in the room but her.

She was poised and slender, with a crown of ash-blonde hair. She was wearing a pretty white eyelet blouse; that much Ben could see from a distance. Was she a teacher with a class? If so, why were they all in church? Clearly, these were not students from the Mary Clokey Porter girls' school. Ben could hardly wait for the service to be over so he could find out more.

At last, Peter Reed and the Egyptian pastor of the church brought the service to a close, and Lydia Reed played the final hymn on the piano. Ben Channing felt himself pulled toward the young woman like a magnet.

He saw the young men being divided into small groups and taken in hand by members of the local Syrian and Armenian Christian communities who worshipped at the Protestant church. Lydia Reed was beside the mystery woman, chatting and smiling. She saw Channing approach.

"Ah, Benjamin! Glad you're here today. I'd like you to meet our guest, Miss Penelope Prior. Penny, this is Benjamin Channing."

The young woman turned her gaze on him, and Ben nearly fell over. Never had he felt so smitten in the presence of a woman. Lovely hazel eyes, soft pale skin, a serious but friendly expression. No words at all came into his mind, so he just nodded and smiled.

"Miss Prior is staying with us for a while. Why don't you come join us for Sunday lunch?" said Mrs. Reed.

The walk from the church to the Reeds' home helped Channing get a grip on himself, so he was fairly coherent by the time their meal was served.

Miss Prior was reticent and soft-spoken, unwilling to volunteer any information about herself. So Peter Reed had to encourage her a bit. "Miss Prior, please explain for Mr. Channing the nature of your work. It's quite fascinating, really. Start from the beginning."

"Well, the beginning . . . I grew up in Tabriz. In northern Persia, where my parents were missionaries. That's where I learned to speak Armenian, you see. During the war, we had to go home to Ohio for a few years. But then, after the war, and after the terrible Armenian deportations from Anatolia, the Near East Relief asked us to return and help the refugees and especially the orphans."

"Over a hundred thousand children, orphaned and displaced. And those are just the ones gathered up and helped by the Near East Relief," Peter said. "There were more than a million refugees in all. One of the most tragic human disasters in history."

"And famine as well," added Miss Prior. "The normal cycles of agriculture were all shattered, so there was terrible hunger. It took millions of dollars in relief and ships full of food to make a start in meeting the need."

"Tell Mr. Channing what you did there," Lydia Reed prompted.

"Oh, I was an Orphanage Assistant. At a place called Kazachi Post. It was an old military barracks that got turned into a shelter for children. In Armenia, near Yerevan."

"That's wonderful, Miss Prior. Such vital work."

"Not wonderful, just basic services. We did whatever we could to help the children. They needed everything: food, clothing, health care, education. I led the sewing classes for girls. My father was a printer, so he made classroom papers and textbooks for the schools. And then, I had to go back to Ohio again." Penelope looked down into her lap, and went silent.

After a pause, Mrs. Reed said, "Mr. Prior died in an accident, in Armenia."

"I am so very sorry," said Ben. "Ohhh my . . . so sorry."

"Yes," whispered Penny.

"But with Miss Prior's experience and skills, she was still needed. So the Near East Relief recruited her again."

"In 1920, though, that's when the Russian Army came to Armenia, and they turned it into a Soviet state," said Penelope. "They let the Near East Relief keep feeding and caring for the refugees—they couldn't manage it themselves. But they didn't want anyone from a missionary background to come in. No more Christian teaching or ministry. They wouldn't allow me to return."

"So what did you do?"

"I was posted to Syria instead. There are many thousands of Armenian refugees there too, of course. People driven south out of Turkey, while the others fled east into the Caucasus. So I got involved with the N.E.R. orphanages in Aleppo, Damascus, and Beirut. I've done that for two years now."

"That still doesn't explain . . . why Tanta? This isn't exactly the center of the world."

"There have always been large communities of Armenians and Syrians in Egypt," Mr. Reed explained. "In Cairo, around the Saint Gregory cathedral, and in Alexandria. Also in Port Said, including some survivors of the siege at Musa Dagh. And Tanta is Egypt's third-largest city, so they are here, too. Most of them are Orthodox and don't come to our church on Sundays."

"But this group that is with me, they are mostly Protestant," said Penny. "We have the great challenge of relocating the orphans who must leave our custody at age sixteen. They need to resettle in a place that has enough Armenians to form a base of support, but not so many that they have trouble finding work opportunities and such. So, Mr. Robertson of the N.E.R. brought the first group of our boys from Syria a few years ago. At first, the Egyptian government didn't want to accept a lot of young men with no families here, thinking they would be rootless and get into mischief. But they did so very well that Egypt has now accepted over 2500 of them, and has even agreed to admit them to full citizenship, which is seldom granted. It's a Near East Relief success story." It was rare for Penny to expend so many words at once, and now she subsided into a bashful silence.

"We have arranged for the Syrians and Armenians at our church to host these boys in their homes and help them get established in Tanta," said Mrs. Reed.

"They need to find jobs and work out their own housing and such, when they are able," Peter Reed said. "It should not take long, because they've already got skills of various kinds, and some English as well, in many cases. We've got a few accountancy clerks, a goldsmith, a couple of builders, a hatmaker, a qualified plumber, and so on."

"Send the plumber over to the Tanta Hospital," Ben suggested. "They're always having trouble with their pipes."

"Good idea."

As they were leaving, Ben found a way to have a private word with Penny.

"Miss Prior, may I call on you here? I'd like to take you through the town a little bit, show you around."

Penny took a moment to reply, causing Ben's heart to constrict. "That would be very kind of you, Mr. Channing," she said, finally.

Ben started breathing again. He waited for a few days, hoping it might be considered a decent interval, then sent word to the Reeds asking permission to stop by. They invited him at once, guessing why he had become so formal all of a sudden.

Benjamin began to take Penny Prior out on simple public excursions. They spent a lot of time strolling around in the Municipal Gardens, where there were two nice fountains that sometimes worked, and many struggling plants and trees. In the fall, the garden was showing the effects of roasting in the summer sun for months. But to Ben, it mattered very little where they went. He was focused on memorizing every inch of Penny Prior, and discovering ways to get her to open up and talk to him.

Penny felt out of her element in Egypt, where she did not speak the language; also, she never expected to be the object of such intense interest. Ben's obvious attraction made her shy and self-conscious. But gradually she learned to accept and trust him.

She asked him many questions about his work at the Borstal and listened attentively to his answers. Whenever she fixed her serious and wide-eyed expression upon him, something inside him melted. He devoted much effort in trying not to make a manifest fool of himself.

Doctor Mourad was fully occupied with his medical work, and with avoiding the members of the cell of the Hassafi Welfare Society who were much too focused on him and his activities.

He had learned that they formed one of many small independent parts of the larger organization affiliated with Hasan al-Banna, who was now a major figure in political Islam in the Delta. He led an increasingly effective popular movement, gradually becoming known as the Muslim Brotherhood.

Their star was rising fast, stimulated by Britain's failures, especially the tragedy in Danasur. They made use of the incident and its dreadful aftermath to bring many new members into their ranks. They spread the message of resistance into the countryside now, to people in villages just like Danasur; before this, their influence had been mainly limited to the *effendi* class in the larger cities.

Their revolutionary base grew wider and more radicalized. It was they who were responsible for some of the attacks upon British soldiers and civil servants. But they were more likely to put pressure on Egyptian professionals like Mourad, whom they regarded as working in support of the foreign and imperialist presence in Egypt. Their aim was not isolated acts of violence, but thorough, sweeping, ideologically-driven social and political change.

Mourad stayed away from the coffee shops he had formerly enjoyed. Sometimes he asked one of the custodians at the Tanta Hospital to go out and do his grocery shopping for him. But keeping a low profile did not insulate him from them, because the organization was bold enough now to seek him out in his apartment, and openly on the street.

"Doctor Mourad, we want to talk to you about your foreign friends. Especially this man called Channing. Don't you know that he is a missionary?

And he is working with boys at the Industrial School, trying to corrupt the minds of our youth."

"Oh, rubbish. He just teaches them to play sports. It's good for them. Healthy. They need to have fun and run around. He's helping them."

"The missionaries always claim to help when they are really exploiting our people for their own purposes. Those boys are prisoners—they can't escape him. Like the sick and the orphans."

"He's not making Christians out of them, if that's what you're worried about," said Mourad. *But he would like to*, he thought. *He would if he could.*

"And now there is another missionary with him. A woman. Who is she?"

"What woman? Mrs. Reed?"

"No, we know about the Reed family. Who is this new woman?"

Mourad was startled by this news. "I really don't know what you mean."

"Don't play games with us. He is your friend. He walks all day in the Gardens with this woman. She is living with the Reeds in their house."

"Well, you are better informed than I am."

"You are not doing a very good job of collecting information for us, Mourad. You don't seem to be trying very hard."

"Sorry," he said acidly, "I'm not trained as a spy. If you don't like my work, get somebody else."

They did not find this amusing. "You will assist us. Who knows, something might happen to those people, wandering around in the Gardens by themselves. They seem to have no regard for their own safety."

Mourad felt a chill throughout his body. They saw that they did not need to say anything more. They turned away and left him.

Ben Channing took the baseball squad out to the big empty lot behind the Mary Clokey Porter School, in the presence of two burly uniformed guards from the Borstal. It was an unusual privilege to be allowed "off grounds," much coveted by the boys, earned through good behavior and performance in their classes.

All of the boys knew that Gamahl Muhammad Faheem had not properly earned this privilege. There was some muttered resentment about his special treatment.

And it was true that Ben had spent as much extra time with this boy as he could. Gamahl was big and physically developed for a fourteen-year-old. His voice had slipped down into an adult register. But he was impulsive and immature, and deeply angry at life in general. He had a permanent bad attitude.

Ben believed that all the young man really needed was some positive attention, patience, and guidance. He believed in modeling the love of Jesus for the least and the lost.

Gamahl showed no sign of appreciation for Ben's well-intended efforts. In fact, Ben's encouraging words and refusal to punish him only seemed to make Gamahl angrier.

The boy's physical strength and coordination ought to have made him well suited to the game of baseball. He could throw straight and fast, and he could hit the ball farther than any other boy. He was like that Little Leaguer who dominates the game because he matures faster than other boys in his age group.

But Gamahl had no interest in learning to play baseball. He didn't really want to be active at all—he had a definite lazy streak to go with his contrary attitude. Out of Channing's earshot, he pronounced Ben a stupid *khawaga* or foreigner, and baseball a stupid *khawaga* game.

That afternoon, Ben wanted to make the most of their training hour, and the other boys were ready and willing.

They started with infield drills. As one boy ran the bases, the others tried to catch the ball and tag him out. Ben threw the ball to each of the infielders, over and over; about half the time they failed to catch it and it rolled away. If they caught it, they could seldom turn and tag in time, before the runner was already on the base. One of their favorite parts of the game was sliding, feet first, into the boy playing second or third, trying to shove him out of contact with the base. This aggressive move sometimes brought out hard feelings, but Ben managed to smooth them over pretty quickly. And since most of the boys were barefoot and Ben was the only one wearing cleats, no physical harm was done.

He then led them in speed-throwing drills. Each boy was supposed to catch the ball in his mitt and shift it to the throwing hand as quickly as possible, then throw it accurately to the next boy. There were, of course, many ways this could go wrong, and they spent a lot of time chasing balls that went anywhere except to the players waiting to catch them.

Finally, they did their batting practice, the boys' favorite part. Ben was the pitcher, and he threw nothing but cupcakes, making it as easy as possible for them to hit the ball. They found the crack of the bat and the flight of the ball very satisfying, and it always ended the practice on a high note, with them all feeling quite accomplished.

Through this entire hour, Gamahl had slumped on the bench, refusing to take part. Not even in the batting practice, at which he normally excelled.

Ben was concerned about him and thought that perhaps he needed some time one-on-one. He conferred with the two guards, and they agreed reluctantly to take the rest of the boys back to the Borstal and leave Ben and Gamahl there alone.

This was a breach of the "off grounds" rules and Ben should have known better.

"Come on, Gamahl, a little batting practice. Move it, on your feet, let's show some energy. You're good at this."

The boy unwillingly got up and into the batter's box. Channing threw him some easy pitches at first, to get him going. Then he began to pitch more seriously, trying to challenge him. Gamahl whiffed a lot of them and became frustrated; the ones he did connect with flew hard and fast into the outfield, impelled by the boy's anger.

"All right, then . . . you seem to be turning your feelings into action. That's a good thing. It's a way to express yourself." Gamahl just stared at Ben like he didn't know what he was talking about. "Let's do some pitching practice. I've told you before, I think you've got what it takes to be a good pitcher. Just send some over the plate here, I'm ready."

Gamahl did have a hard, smooth ball delivery, and quite accurate. But that meant almost all of his pitches were fastballs. Ben knew what to expect and it was easy for him to turn the force of the pitch into the force of the hit. He kept batting them off toward the wall at the edge of the American Mission property.

This upset Gamahl as well, and he sent one straight toward Ben, forcing him to twist out of the way and take the pitch below his left shoulderblade. "Ouch! Okay, Gamahl . . . I've seen pitchers do that when they get annoyed . . . it happens. Let's try to work on your technique a little bit."

Ben dragged out a wooden pitching guide he had asked the woodshop to build for him. It was like an empty picture frame on legs, locating the edges of the strike zone. He went out and stood with Gamahl, facing the plate.

"If you're going to throw anything but fastballs, you need to learn to control the ball's spin. Try putting your fingers against the seams on the ball, and when you release it, move your wrist a little, like this. And maybe you'll get a curveball." Ben sent a pitch through the wooden frame. "Well, just try it. It's kind of fun to find ways to make the ball move but still end up in the right place." They worked on this for a while. Ben was absorbed in the curveball question and lost track of the time. Finally, Gamahl let out a disgusted sigh and went off to collapse on the bench as if Ben had tried him to the breaking point.

"Oh man, it must be getting late. You want to help me gather up our stuff?" said Ben, offering him a *shanta* bag. Gamahl ignored him. "Okay, I'll just go and get the baseballs." Ben went to the outfield to pick up all of the balls strewn around after batting practice.

In the meantime, the guards who had taken the other boys back to the Borstal became uneasy about what they had done, and went to report it to Mr. Fauber. Understandably, Fauber was not happy about it. He went over to the playing field himself to straighten them out.

He found Gamahl lounging on the bench while his coach was out there doing the cleanup alone. Furthermore, Gamahl refused to stand when Mr. Fauber addressed him, as the rules required. "On your feet, boy! Stand when I speak to you!" he shouted.

"*Kuss ummak,*" the boy snarled.

This was an expression so foul that even Fauber was taken aback, after a career in youth incarceration. He suddenly brimmed over with rage.

Channing looked back at the plate to see Fauber seize a baseball bat and begin to beat Gamahl on his legs and shoulders. Both of them were shouting and swearing. "No! NO! Mr. Fauber! NO!" he yelled. He ran toward the plate, which somehow seemed to be miles away.

He saw Gamahl wrench the bat away from Fauber and swing it at him, striking him on the neck. Fauber fell down upon his hands and knees in the dust and blood flowed from his mouth.

Channing struggled to lift Fauber from the ground, turned to look at Gamahl, and for the first time saw a slight smile on the boy's face.

Mr. Fauber was taken to the Tanta Hospital. And Benjamin Channing was taken to the Al-Mudiriya Prison.

In the south of town, beside the primary train station, stood the extensive regional complex that included the offices of the Gharbiya provincial government, the courthouses, and the holding cells for those charged with serious crimes. Tanta's central Post Office, the Agriculture Authority, and the Fire Brigade occupied the same neighborhood.

Egypt's court system was a relic of the Ottoman era, with a super-structure of French and British colonial influences. There were the Islamic religious courts, which decided issues of family and personal status, marriage, inheritance, and the like. There were the Native Courts, which settled disputes involving Egyptians only. There were the Consular Courts, set up by the representatives of foreign countries to regulate the behavior of their own nationals, based upon the special privileges accorded by treaty under the Capitulations established by Constantinople and the Turkish Sultan. And there were the Mixed Courts, with jurisdiction over conflicts between Egyptian citizens and persons from other countries.

The result was a bewildering jumble of statutes and ordinances that provided secure employment for many, many members of the legal profession.

Ben Channing had absolutely no knowledge of the Egyptian legal system and had never for a moment imagined that he would have any need to know about it. But here he was, sitting alone in a jail cell, wondering what on earth was going on.

After what might have been a day and a night and another day—but seemed much longer—his cell was opened and he was taken to an interrogation room, where he found Peter Reed and another man waiting for him. At first he was overjoyed to see Peter, but then realized that Reed's face was very closed and his manner stiff and distant. Peter introduced the man accompanying him.

"This is Mr. Bradley, representing the American Legation in Cairo. He is here to serve as your legal advisor."

"I'm not sure why I need a legal advisor. I don't understand what I'm doing here."

"Mr. Channing, you are accused of a very serious offense," said Mr. Bradley. "Under Title Two, Chapter One, Part Two, Article Nine of the Penal Code, officers of justice may be charged with a felony if they are found to have violated the law while in the performance of their duties, or through an abuse of their powers. This category includes assault upon private individuals. The offense is aggravated if the victim is a minor."

"You've already lost me. I didn't assault anyone. And I'm not a police officer."

"The Tanta Industrial School is a part of the state apparatus of law and order, under the administration of the Bureau of Prisons. Mr. Jeremy

Fauber is your immediate supervisor, and he is an employee of the Bureau of Prisons. You are understood to be acting under his authority."

"I'm a volunteer. I work for the American Mission in Egypt."

"Mr. Bradley is aware of that," said Peter Reed. "But it doesn't change the fact that at the school you are functioning as a member of the prison administration."

"I also don't understand what you mean by assault. What do they think I did?"

"A young inmate of the Industrial School, Gamahl Muhammad Faheem, was assaulted on the playground. He states that you and Mr. Fauber were responsible."

Ben shook his head firmly. "No, that's not what happened. I swear to you that I never laid a hand on that boy. Never would I do that, not in a million years. I swear it." Channing paused. "It's true that Fauber did, though."

"The boy claims that you both beat him. With a baseball bat. And that you did it because he refused to become a Christian."

Ben gaped at them. A huge chasm seemed to open in front of him. "That's not true. Gamahl is lying. Why?! Oh Lord, why?"

"I can think of a number of possible reasons, and I believe that is the direction we shall be going in your defense," Bradley said. "One of those reasons may be that in a recent case in the Mixed Courts, it was found and upheld on appeal that persons acting for the state may be personally liable for malfeasance or negligence. That means you might have to pay compensation to the victim for injuries sustained."

Benjamin was staggered by all of this, and its implications. Most of all, he was hurt by Gamahl's lie. Ben had scrupulously avoided mentioning anything about Jesus or the Christian faith to Gamahl, believing that if he behaved toward the boy in a forbearing, Christlike way, the boy would ask him about it himself when he was ready. Gamahl's statement was a bold, malicious, dangerous lie.

"It's just false," he said, meekly. "I didn't do it. I wouldn't do it."

"There is another witness," said Mr. Bradley. "A man by the name of Husni Uthman. He apparently shares an apartment with you and several other teachers."

"What?! Husni?"

"Mr. Uthman also works at the Industrial School. He says you told him that you were trying to induce the boy Gamahl to convert to Christianity."

Ben felt that he must be losing his mind. "No . . . I never talked to him about any such thing. Why would he say that?"

Mr. Bradley frowned, and glanced at Mr. Reed. "We suspect political motives. There is some indication that Husni Uthman may be a member of a sort of underground radical Islamic group. They call it the Muslim Brotherhood. It seems that they want to use this case to undermine all Christian missionaries in Egypt."

Benjamin was speechless.

"It's an ugly business, Ben," said Peter Reed. "We are beginning to think that this whole incident might have been planned, as a provocation. It certainly is being deployed right now as a weapon against us. Not just here in Tanta . . . all over the country."

"Very difficult to prove, however," observed Mr. Bradley. "If there is some larger conspiracy."

"It's an enormous scandal, already, in any event," added Peter. "It doesn't need to be true to cause an explosion in the Egyptian press."

"Oh, dear God," Benjamin whispered.

They sat silently for a few minutes. Then Mr. Bradley said, "Due to the political pressure, I expect this case to move rather quickly. There is an arraignment scheduled for Monday. Mr. Fauber will be tried separately once he has recovered from his wounds. I think you can expect to stay here during proceedings, since they will argue against granting bail."

"Are you all right, Ben?" asked Peter, his voice softening. "Can we bring you anything?"

"Ohhh . . . uhhhh . . . will they let me have books? Writing paper . . . I need to tell my mother something. Maybe some fruit."

"We'll do what we can," Peter said. "Mr. Bradley, would you excuse us for just a moment, please?"

"Certainly," Bradley said, and left the room.

"I wanted to tell you," Peter began. "Penelope Prior has been asking about you. Well, more than that, really. She's quite distraught. She wants to come here herself, but of course they are not going to allow that. I think . . . the arraignment is in open court . . . but I think I'm going to persuade her not to come. It all might be a bit too upsetting for her."

"Yes," said Ben. "I think so, too. But please . . . give her my best regards."

"I'll do that. And know that all of us are praying for you." Ben felt that he should reply to this in some polite manner . . . but he was unable to do it.

Only a few months after the Danasur debacle, the Tanta incident blasted through the Egyptian press. All competitors in the information marketplace wanted to outdo the others in their condemnation of the British prison system and its mistreatment of defenseless youth. And thanks to Ben's involvement, they could also go after the Christian missionaries, who were viewed by many as the imperial order's willing partners.

All sorts of assertions were made in print that had little to do with the facts. And these claims were quickly passed by word of mouth throughout every level of society.

The highly influential newspaper *Al-Manar* printed a categorical rejection of the concept of a separation between religion and state. "This idea is nothing but a degenerate innovation, a *bidaa*," they wrote. "It is clearly meant only to weaken Islam and the Egyptian people, and to make them easier to control. We ought to have one law in Egypt, and only one: *sharia* law, which should apply to Christians and to other non-Muslim minorities, just as has been done successfully for centuries in properly administered Muslim lands. There should be no such thing as the Mixed Courts. Muslims should be the ones to adjudicate issues involving foreigners in their midst, and Muslims must do so according to *sharia*. For it is Muslims alone who hold the word of truth, and all others must be subject to it, as Allah himself requires."

Another writer agreed. "The British, French, and Dutch imperialists, their Orientalist scholars, and all Christian missionaries seek only to destroy Muslim values and morale, in all of the places they wrongfully inhabit. From North Africa to Southeast Asia, we must root out these occupiers and reject their influence. Send them packing out of our sacred lands!"

"Anglo-American missionaries are nothing but duplicitous imperialist agents. They wish to incite communal discord," wrote another. "Evangelism today is a twentieth-century Crusade, using the weapons of schoolbooks and shelters and scalpels instead of the lances and arrows of old. We must speak out against it in all mosque sermons, teaching the people to protect themselves. We must close all missionary schools and other institutions. We must criminalize all preaching by the enemies of our faith. We must strengthen the work of our own evangelism, of Islamic *daawa*, in a worldwide mission to present and promote our divine truth."

"The foreign liars can only succeed by trickery, for we know that the Quran is the sole source of the knowledge of Allah. They have corrupted and distorted their own holy books and they intend to neutralize ours."

"The Christians are infidels who have always hated our pure religion. Muslims must expel them from the House of Islam. They belong only to the House of War. We have every right to kill them in our lands unless they accept their subordinate status as powerless minorities. We should do to them what they have done to us, at Danasur and Tanta and countless other places. Indeed, the strife will continue until the Christian West is forced to acknowledge the authority of the Prophet Muhammad, and our religion rules over all."

"Take not as your friends the Christians and Jews. Befriend them not, trust them not, O Muslims; they are your enemies. They must only be defeated."

"Some say that individuals should have the right to accept Christianity if they wish to. No, my brothers, I tell you this is false," wrote the editor of a publication with ties to the Muslim Brotherhood. "The converts are being misled by the missionaries—they are not freely choosing. They are being coerced through bribery and propaganda and even by brute force. How can a child choose to betray his religion or be beaten with a block of wood?"

Then the Tanta Sharia Court decided to weigh in on this issue. They formally declared that any convert from Islam to Christianity was an apostate. He must be offered the option to return to Islam or be stoned to death in the market square. This demand went so far as to shock and dismay the Western-educated and more secular Egyptians who suspected that they would be targeted next. There was a rather fine line, after all, between those who could be called "apostate" and those who wished to read and believe and think for themselves, not following the Islamic authorities. The sheikhs seldom knew anything except their own traditional lore, and had no regard whatsoever for the learning and the independent thought of others.

Some Egyptians, such as the feminist leader Huda Shaarawi, who had been struggling against Islamic chauvinism all her life, were incensed by the conservative reaction. With her Western education and her Western friends, she felt it was more than possible to live in the world as an enlightened Muslim.

When the Tanta incident struck, Huda Shaarawi was in Europe, representing the Egyptian Feminist Union with two compatriots, at the meeting of the International Women's Suffrage Alliance in Rome.

Over two thousand women participated, from numerous countries. They discussed equality in wages and employment, married women's individual rights, legal issues affecting women, and of course, enfranchisement.

Huda and her friends wore Western clothing and went unveiled; they spoke French and moved around the city with great freedom. The Asian and African women were the special stars of the event, giving many press interviews. The European papers viewed their presence as an indictment of the allegedly backward societies from which they came.

The three Egyptian women sailed from Brindisi to Alexandria at the close of the conference, assuming their traditional garb on the ship. They went on from Alexandria to Cairo by train, where they expected to be met by photographers and reporters. When the train arrived, they made sure that the reporters were ready, and that a crowd of women from their organization was waiting to meet them. Then they stepped out from the train car and—in front of everyone—pulled off the white *yashmak* veils covering their faces, and tossed them away.

There was a moment of surprise, and then the other women waiting on the platform did the same, waving their veils in the air and hooting with joy. Huda gave an interview on the spot that managed to make Egypt's Islamic reactionaries even more furious than they already were.

The Tanta case was taking on such a high profile that the Minister of Justice himself, Boutros Ghobrial, decided to come to Tanta from Cairo to confer with the judges likely to hear the case, and with the provincial Governor, Rifaat Bey. Lord Mosby deputized Charles Coles, the Inspector-General for Prisons in Egypt, to represent the interests of the Empire.

Boutros Ghobrial was the same Justice Minister who had presided over the military tribunal that tried and sentenced the hapless villagers of Danasur.

"I think we can agree that the press coverage of this case is hopelessly biased and inaccurate, even libelous," said the Minister. "The French-language papers are perhaps the worst."

"The reptile press," said Coles Pasha with scorn. "They are using this incident as proof that the power of England is wielded without regard for the welfare of the people, with the sole object of furthering our own political and commercial interests. I say, I say! After all that we have done for them! The youth corrections system in particular, my special pride! The reformatories at Giza and Tanta are as advanced as any in Europe."

"It seems there were some errors made, however," said Governor Rifaat Bey.

"Mere slander, I am altogether certain. Obviously the true nature of British influence is not to impose an uncongenial foreign system upon a reluctant people, but rather to enable the triumph of the ideals of humanity and justice. These people are convinced that they could better achieve this by themselves, or at least that they are now able to carry it on by themselves, without our continuing guidance. It's a nonsensical effusion of confidence, to be sure." Coles Pasha might have forgotten that the two officials with whom he was speaking were themselves Egyptians.

"But it seems clear that there was a violation of order in the handling of this inmate," the Governor insisted.

"Probably due to lenience or permissiveness by administrators," suggested the Justice Minister. "They allowed him too many privileges. That only leads to a truculent defiance of authority. One must suppress all lawlessness and effrontery without mercy."

"As they did at Danasur?" said the Governor pointedly, receiving cold stares from his two colleagues. "Listen to me. The reaction among the press and the public is dangerous. I believe widespread civil disorder is quite possible. To be clear, I have no personal feelings in this matter. I don't care if the entire province of Gharbiya embraces any religion they want to. But I do care if everything blows up into chaos and violence."

Their meeting continued, striving to figure out how to deal with this controversy in the most effective manner, at least from their points of view.

When they were ready to leave the Governorate office, they came down the front steps, still talking, moving toward their carriages. At that point, Coles heard a sharp sound, and turned toward Boutros Ghobrial. He saw a great bloody blotch spreading where the man's left eye ought to be. Other bullets hit the cobbled pavement where they were standing, and everyone present began to run or crouch upon the ground.

The sniper managed to kill only one of them that day. But his message had clearly been sent. In the disarray that followed, Benjamin Channing's arraignment was indefinitely postponed.

Chapter 9

Enclosed in his windowless cell, Ben had no notion of the passage of time. The only light in his cell came from a long slit above the door, one brick wide, letting in light from the corridor, where electric bulbs burned round the clock. Guards would come and go, food would appear, his chamber pot would be taken away.

He tried to chat with the guards in a sociable manner, just as he did with everyone, everywhere. But apparently they had orders not to talk to him. Solitary confinement for a friendly, caring person was really rather cruel, and he found himself getting very discouraged.

Then one of the guards brought him a written message in an unsealed envelope. Ben was so obviously happy to get it that the guard departed from his orders enough to celebrate with him, with smiles and a joyful "*Mabruk!*" Congratulations!

On the envelope was written "Mr. Benjamin Channing." He opened it and found just a small slip of paper.

Dear Benjamin,

> *Mr. Bradley says that I may send a short note. He says that any long letter will not be approved.*
> *Ben, I am so sorry that you are going through this difficult trial. It is so frightening, and so* xxxxxx [here she had written the word "unjust," which was crossed out by the prison censor]. *I wish to send you a certain Scripture, especially for you. Here it is:*

> > *Trust in the Lord with all thine heart*
> > *And lean not unto thine own understanding.*
> > *In all thy ways acknowledge Him*
> > *And He shall make straight thy path.*

*I am sure that you recognize Proverbs 3:5–6. Ben, I would
come and visit you, but Mr. Bradley says it is not allowed. So please
just be well and be strong, and also be very sure that I am thinking
of you.*

   May God bless you and keep you safe . . .
   Your friend Penelope Prior

Poor Ben was so elated by this simple missive that he reread it a hundred times a day. He was still waiting for them to permit him to have writing paper, so he was not even able to reply. But he asked the Lord in his prayers to let her know how much it meant to him.

Another period of gloomy days went by. Then his cell door opened.

"Mourad! Oh thank the Lord, it's so good to see you!"

"Oh yes," Mourad replied. "But please, don't get too excited. I only got permission to come here because I am your doctor and I could prove that you have been under my care for a life-threatening pulmonary condition. So, a little coughing would be appropriate."

Ben tried to oblige with a realistic-sounding bout of coughs.

The door of his cell was left open with two guards blocking the passage, watching them and listening to their conversation.

"And remember, we are not allowed to discuss your case in any way. Only your present condition."

"To be honest, I'm all right. Just very alone."

"Meals? Are they feeding you properly?"

"Bread and *fule*. A fellow can survive on that."

"Well, I am authorized to give you these," said Mourad, handing over a sack of oranges.

"Thank you! I do appreciate it."

"I have also brought you all of the novels I still have from my Asyut College days. Here you are. Fortunately they are long ones." From his large bag he brought out copies in English of *Phantom of the Opera*, *The Count of Monte Cristo*, *A Tale of Two Cities*, and *Les Miserables*. "Apparently your jailors are not aware that most of these stories center upon a person unjustly imprisoned . . . and even one unjustly executed, I am sorry to say. Perhaps I should have reconsidered the Dickens."

"No, no, I am desperate for something to read. I don't even have a Bible."

Mourad looked surprised. "What? That's atrocious. I'm sure that's against regulations. I shall complain for you. Unfortunately I did not bring one."

"Never mind."

"No, that is not acceptable. I shall ask Peter Reed to send one."

"Thank you."

"Also, I have brought you a stack of clean things from your apartment. Only socks and underclothes. You are required to wear those prison-issue tunics and trousers, so I can't bring you any other clothing. Not even your baseball uniform."

"Mourad! How could you? That's not funny."

"Please take off your shirt now, and let's have some more coughing, if you please. I need to look as though I am examining your lungs. And in fact, I would rather like to know that you haven't picked up some contagion in here."

"Perhaps fleas," said Ben wearily.

"I do see some red insect bites. They need to allow you to wash."

"What I want to do is go back to my apartment and wash properly," said Ben.

"Ahhh, there is news about your apartment. I must explain it without mentioning certain names, in case our listeners are waiting to hear them. When we learned about the actions of that Judas, you know who I mean, your friends at the flat went into his room, dragged out all of his belongings, and threw them into the stairwell. Then they sat on the stairs and waited for him. When he came home, they made him give up his keys in exchange for his clothes, and told him he was out of the flat and should never return. They are upset about this, your friends. As he was leaving, even old Saad the doorkeeper actually spat on him."

"Saad is my friend, too," Ben said innocently.

"Of course he is. Don't forget how many allies you have out there in the somewhat more real world."

"Mourad . . . I know that you are trying to cheer me up, and it's very kind of you. But actually, I regret the way they treated him," Ben said, speaking in a low voice. "We don't know if he intended to hurt me. Maybe he felt forced to do that, somehow. Maybe he blurted out something without thinking. It can be very intimidating to find yourself interrogated by the police . . . maybe he made a mistake, I don't know. Even if he did it out of loyalty to a cause, that's somewhat understandable too. Anyway, what I want to say is that I have forgiven him, from my heart. And I'm sorry they did that."

Mourad looked at Ben's face and his facetious manner fell away.

"Also the boy . . . I can't say his name either, I guess," Ben continued. "I have forgiven him, too. Imagine what he must have been through in his short life to hold so much anger in his heart. I've been spending a lot of time praying for him."

"Really?"

"Oh yes. You know, one thing about not having a Bible in here is that I've had to dig deep into my memory and pull out Scripture to think about. And what keeps coming to my mind are the words of Jesus from the Gospels. Jesus said it so clearly: 'Love your enemies and pray for them that despitefully use you . . . bless them that curse you, do good to them that hate you . . . if you love those who love you, what reward have ye? Do not even the sinners do the same?' I mean, he didn't just command us to love our friends. But also those who hurt us."

"Seems . . . unrealistic."

"Well yes, it does go against our natural inclinations. But I'll tell you something else I've discovered: the longing of Christ is to *save*. To *bless*. Not to punish or reject. To save and to bless. That's what he wants, more than anything. And if he is in your heart, you too are filled with that desire. I wish that right now I could offer his love and forgiveness to them. For God so loved the world that he sent his Son to bring us life . . . and if God did not send Jesus into the world to condemn it, I doubt very much that he sent me to do it instead."

"How can you forgive someone who hasn't apologized? And doesn't intend to?"

"I've had a lot of empty hours in here to search my own soul and my conscience. I've had to ask the Lord to forgive me for all kinds of things. Mourad, you know the prayer that Jesus taught: 'Forgive us our sins, as we forgive those who sin against us.' No exceptions, no conditions. That's what he taught. Whether I like it or not."

Mourad was not sure how to respond.

Ben could not let it go. He had been alone for several weeks now without talking to anyone. "Jesus even forgave his killers from the cross. Not sure I could go that far. I'm not even able to forgive those who killed my friend Mikhail—sorry, maybe I shouldn't have spoken his name—in the village. Or that other poor soul who was just passing by and tried to help. The death of innocents is just too hard to accept."

"Time's up," said one of the guards, tired of listening to a conversation he could not comprehend.

"Yes, just a moment, please," Mourad said. "Ben, deep breathing now, let me listen to that lung." He placed his stethoscope carefully on Channing's chest and back. "All right, that sounds clear. You may have problems, but pneumonia is no longer one of them."

"Thank you for coming, Mourad. Please give my best to the fellows at the flat."

Mourad placed his hand on Ben's shoulder.

"No touching," said the guard.

"Yes, all right," replied Mourad. "Goodbye for now, Ben. See you soon, *inshah allah*." God willing.

Mourad kept thinking about his brief conversation with Benjamin. He had been required to attend chapel services and Christian instruction while he was a student at Asyut College. But he had never paid much attention to it, since he assumed it did not apply to him.

But something was working in the quiet corners of his mind. He began to wonder what he had missed, years ago. Surprised by his own behavior, he went to the Tanta Hospital chaplain, Rev. Gayyid, and asked to borrow an Arabic Bible.

He knew enough to realize that it was the New Testament where he would find information about Jesus. So he began to read, starting at the Gospel of Matthew.

He came across the very passage Ben had quoted, about loving one's enemies. And a great deal more, besides.

Mourad was screening pulmonary cases at the outpatient clinic when he suddenly found himself face to face with the leader of the Islamist cell who had been pressuring him for reports on his colleagues and friends. But this time, Mourad felt not fear, but something very different.

"You've got some nerve showing up here," he said.

"Doctor Mourad, you have been to visit the missionary Channing at the prison. Tell me everything that happened there."

"I shall tell you nothing. Not now, not ever. What I do is none of your business and you can just leave me alone."

"Your friend is in a very vulnerable spot. We have allies at the prison."

"I'm through listening to your threats. *Ya metnaak!*" he snapped, using a very unprofessional obscenity. "Get out of my clinic and don't ever come near me again." The man shot him a contemptuous look, but he did go away.

Mourad had plenty of time to doubt himself later. Was that bravado dangerous and unwise? Perhaps his scorn had been just another manifestation of fear. Why was it that Ben Channing seemed so calm under pressure? He was so very young, only twenty-three years old. Where did his patience and charity come from? Was it merely naïve? Mourad reflected on the fact that it was quite possible to be heroic and misguided at the same time.

Mourad continued to read through the Gospel of Matthew. Jesus too seemed to have an annoying tendency to accept abuse, even betrayal, from other people. No Muslim would behave like that, at least in his experience. Why had he never noticed any of this before?

He spent an exhausting day providing patient care while fretting and simmering under the surface.

That night in his apartment, he was more than ready for sleep, but too wound up to relax. After tossing and turning for a long while, he finally dropped off. He awoke abruptly to the sound of someone gasping aloud, then realized that it was his own voice. He felt a wave of terror unlike anything he had experienced before, his body alerting him urgently to a "fight or flight" response, yet he was unable to move at all. His arms and legs were completely unresponsive. He was helpless. Only his eyes were able to move, and they detected a faint presence in a corner of the room, a shadow or a dark shape. But something told him clearly that it was not human.

As he lay there trapped and gasping, he began to perceive more of the shadowy shapes, surrounding his bed, slowly moving closer.

Then the sense of immobility left him, and he thrashed himself fully awake. What kind of a diabolical dream was that? As a physician, he was aware of the phenomenon of sleep paralysis, in which movement of the body was suppressed by the brain during sleep. But he was not aware that one could be partly awake, dreaming, yet still paralyzed.

Was this the start of a psychosis of some kind? He considered going to consult his colleague and mentor, Dr. Philip Hessburgh. But he was vaguely ashamed of his mental condition and reluctant to reveal it to him.

He picked up his Quran, roughly remembering something in it about meaningful dreams. He found the Surah *Yusuf*, with all of those verses about the seven fat cows and the seven lean cows, and so on. Mourad would have been happy to dream about cows instead of the horror he had just experienced.

Then he found on his bookshelf a collection of *hadith* narratives that he had received as a gift years ago. These were sayings and brief stories from the life of the Prophet Muhammad and his early Companions, meant to serve as a guide to the behavior of believers in their daily life. It took him a while to understand how the book was organized, but eventually he came upon several entries about sleeping, including this one: "A good vision or *ruya* is from Allah and a bad dream or *hulm* is from Satan." A sentiment that reassured him not at all.

A few days later, Benjamin Channing was brought out of his cell again and into the interrogation room, where he found Peter Reed and the American Consulate lawyer, Mr. Bradley.

Peter took a good look at Channing and responded with concern. "Ben . . . you are evidently not quite yourself. Are you being mistreated?"

"No . . . not mistreated exactly. Not beaten or anything. But I think they are skipping meals . . . I am often very hungry and thirsty. And they have taken away the things Doctor Mourad brought to me, even though he got permission to bring them, beforehand. They took away the books, and the oranges, and the clean clothes. It's a little depressing."

"What about the things I brought you? The food, and the Bible, and other books?"

"I never got those. I didn't know you had brought them."

Peter shook his head, and Mr. Bradley said, "That is a policy violation. I shall look into a formal consular protest. I am very sorry, Mr. Channing."

"I'm surviving," said Ben.

"At least we can bring you some good news. There have been developments in your case. The most significant is that Mr. Jeremy Fauber has confessed to the assault upon Gamahl Muhammad and declared himself fully accountable. He has offered sworn evidence that you were not to blame."

"What?"

"They've now got a no-contest case. They don't need you anymore," said Peter.

"The fact is that they don't do any real police work, here," said Bradley with uncharacteristic frankness. "What they do is try to get the accused to confess, and then the case is considered solved, closed, done with. Fauber has pleaded guilty and is to be expelled from the country. But he has not implicated you in the assault."

"God bless you, Mr. Fauber," said Ben.

"Let's not forget that his rash behavior caused this whole scandal to begin with," said Peter angrily. "What he did was inexcusable."

"He lost his temper, Peter. It could happen to anyone. Gamahl did go out of his way to provoke him."

"And now he will go home, no doubt to a range of job offers from a lot of Borstals in Britain. He's a hero to some. Made these bloody wogs show proper respect."

"He failed. It was a moment of failure, and now he's trying to set it right," Ben said. "I mean, it could also be seen that way."

"There is further news," said Mr. Bradley. "The second witness, Mr. Husni Uthman, has recanted his testimony."

"He has?"

"Yes, he says he was mistaken. Misunderstood you, or something. He suggests that he was under the influence of others, who confused him. Not a very convincing statement, but again, it simplifies things, which from the point of view of the investigating magistrates is good. They are likely to accept that."

"Last I heard," added Peter, "he had decided to go and teach school in Riyadh, or Bahrain, or somewhere."

"I hope he'll be okay," said Ben.

"So, *in toto*, there are reasons for encouragement," said Bradley. "We are asking you to be patient a little while longer."

"You know what I think is odd?" said Ben. "Mr. Zwemer hasn't been here to see me. Isn't that his responsibility, as acting head of the American Mission?"

"All right, that was me," said Peter Reed. "I told him that his presence here would be counterproductive. In view of his widely known advocacy of conversions to Christianity from Islam. We've already got a problem in that area—we don't need to make it worse."

"I never tried to convert that boy. I can't imagine where Gamahl got all of that. Did someone influence him, too?"

"We don't know. He is being very uncooperative. If not for his accusations, you'd probably be released. The panel of judges will have to decide whether his uncorroborated evidence is enough to charge you."

Ben felt suddenly very tired. "Thank you," he said in a hushed voice.

"I shall see about the things you should have been allowed to have," said Bradley. "For whatever reason, someone is withholding them. That is unacceptable."

Benjamin merely nodded, and sighed.

Why was conversion such a sensitive subject in Muslim countries? Because departing from the religion of your origin was not viewed as a personal choice that any individual might make. It was a repudiation of your social identity, your home and your people.

More than that, an essential tenet of Islam held that the Quran was the direct, verbatim, final revelation of God, encompassing and superseding any revelations before it. Therefore, leaving Islam and sliding backwards into an earlier faith could only be considered apostasy. Individuals were encouraged to embrace Islam, but never to depart from it—a fatal error.

It was fatal in very literal terms for many. The family and community of any convert were shamed by his deviant behavior and would do almost anything to deter him. Threats, beatings, rejection, divorce, and disinheritance were common; the individual could lose his home and his job and be fully ostracized by his neighbors. There were instances of converts being kidnapped and held captive until they changed their minds. A woman or girl could be compelled to marry a Muslim man and accept his authority. Sometimes, the dishonor was felt to be so great that killing the convert seemed the only solution. Several very public murders of known converts took place in Egypt.

Muslim police, judges, and officials turned a blind eye to this vigilantism. British colonial authorities valued stability above all, certainly above personal rights or freedoms; they were determined to prevent communal conflict and refused to intervene.

Every missionary knew secret Christians, "hidden believers" who were not ready to declare themselves publicly. But this could be a painful way to live, and even indigenous Christians harbored some mistrust of those who might be informers in their midst.

The cost of Christian discipleship in Egypt was indeed very great. And missionaries without tact or wisdom could easily make it greater.

Mourad Wahba was aware of all this. He even had personal knowledge of individuals in Asyut who had tried to migrate quietly into the Christian faith and found their lives imperiled by chaos and discord. Only a fool would court disaster like that.

He told himself that the smart thing to do would be to stop reading the Bible at once and put all of these bewildering thoughts out of his mind, forever.

That night, he awoke in a state of terror with the feeling of a huge weight pressing upon his chest and his throat tightening, like someone was choking him. He could scarcely breathe. Again, he felt paralyzed, his limbs useless. Before his eyes, he saw a cloud of dark smoke coalesce into the shape of a black demon sitting on his chest, strangling him with its paws, exhaling fumes into his face. It seemed entirely, physically, concretely real.

Then he felt another presence beside the bed. It was the figure of a man, dignified and regal. With the exaggerated clarity that sometimes happens in dreams, he saw that the man's robe was made out of tiny glittering pieces of silvery metal, not like normal clothing at all. Upon his head he wore a silver band like a crown, shiny as a mirror. Mourad could see him only with peripheral vision, unable to turn his head.

The man swung his arm out in front of Mourad and dispelled the creature into smoke again. Then the dream disappeared and Mourad was fully awake.

This was just a little too much. In the morning he went straight to Philip Hessburgh's office.

"Excuse me, Doctor . . . I've got a patient who is complaining of sleep paralysis, with shortness of breath. I'm not sure whether this is a psychiatric disorder. Can you direct me to information on this?"

Dr. Hessburgh scanned his bookshelves quickly. "Actually, I do have something here . . . I can almost remember where it is. Oh yes, I think this is it." He pulled out a book called *Insomnia: Its Causes and Treatment* by Sir James Sawyer, published in Birmingham in 1912. "I'm pretty sure there is something about it in here."

"Thank you."

"I'm sorry, I'm in a hurry just now—surgery in ten minutes—but if you'd like to discuss it later, please come back. I'm no expert in sleep disorders but I'll examine the patient if you wish."

"I'll read up on it first," Mourad said, quickly leaving the room.

Sir James Sawyer told Mourad that sleep paralysis was not uncommon in a semi-waking state. And hallucinations were a distinctive feature of the condition. They fell into three major categories: vestibular sensations, as of falling or spinning; intruder effects, with the sense of a vague threatening presence in the room; and the incubus phenomenon, in which pressure on the chest and difficulty breathing became associated with an evil being or demonic creature.

"Lucky me," said Mourad. "At least I don't have the vertigo yet."

Unfortunately, Dr. Sawyer had no advice for treating the condition, except for calming the patient and relieving his or her sense of anxiety. Mourad thought that was unlikely to happen.

Ben was called for another interview with Peter Reed and Mr. Bradley.

"Mr. Channing, let me get right to the point: you are about to be released," Bradley said. "The members of the panel of inquiry, with the approval of the acting Minister of Justice, have decided not to charge you. The case is dismissed."

Ben dropped into a chair. "Thank you, Lord," he muttered.

"There isn't enough evidence that you were actually involved in the altercation. And Mr. Fauber's testimony outweighed the victim's because he stood to gain nothing by it. That's what they wrote in their opinion."

"We're very happy for you, Ben," said Peter sincerely.

"Some conditions do apply," said Mr. Bradley. "I'm sorry to say that your residence permit and work permit have been revoked. You've been given two weeks to leave the country. That also terminates your position with the American Mission in Egypt."

Ben merely blinked as if he did not know how to react to this.

"If I may," said Peter Reed. "We've been anticipating this, and we've made some enquiries on your behalf. You've been offered a position in Syria with the Near East Relief, doing refugee support. Your growing fluency in Arabic should be of great value there."

A pause followed, as this news penetrated Channing's mind. Then he suddenly stood up again.

"In Syria? With the Near East Relief?"

"Yes, that's what I said," replied Peter, smiling.

All three of them were embarrassed at this point when Ben Channing crumbled into tears. They waited in silence while Benjamin wept. Peter Reed gave him a clean handkerchief.

"We'll do whatever we can to help you settle your affairs here," said Mr. Bradley.

Ben nodded, mopping his face. Then he stopped and said, "There is something you could do for me. I'd like to consult with you about it as soon as I'm out of here."

"I'm at your service," Bradley confirmed.

"Can you please tell me how long I've actually been here?" Ben asked.

"You've been at the Al-Mudiriya Prison in solitary confinement for six weeks."

"That doesn't sound like very long," said Ben. "But ohhhh, it is."

"It's behind you, now," said Peter. "And it seems there are better things to come." This comment made Benjamin weep again.

After Mourad's research into sleep paralysis, he had another dream.

This time, he saw himself not in bed, but kneeling on a prayer rug. As he recited the *salat*, he was conscious again of the shadowy shapes on the edges of his room, moving slowly closer to him. *You are only an intruder hallucination*, he thought, in a semi-lucid state.

Then suddenly he was no longer in his room, but kneeling on the ground in a dry, barren landscape. Before him lay an open vista of lifeless reddish dust and rocks, flat all the way to the horizon. It could have been the surface of Mars.

Then he became aware of the shining silvery figure standing in front of him. There was a rippling effect in the air that made it hard to see him clearly. But Mourad's mind spoke the single word, *Isa*. Jesus. And his own mind replied, *Jesus doesn't look like that. I've seen pictures.* Nevertheless, he knew that is who it was.

The regal figure never said a word, but Mourad got an overwhelming sense of benign power.

The figure stepped closer, and leaned down over him. With one fingertip, he touched the top of Mourad's head. A crack appeared where he was touched, and the skin began to split. Sheets of skin came loose and rolled back like paper, falling away from his body. And Mourad realized with a sense of horror that under his skin, there was a shadowy shape like the ones haunting his room. His skin was an empty shell containing only a dark mass of nothingness.

He gasped and emitted a guttural cry, and woke himself up.

"Lord Isa!" he cried aloud. "O Prophet! What are you doing to me? Why are you besetting me with *djinn* and phantasms? Please, have mercy on me!"

Then Mourad felt submerged in a sea of peace. A soft, liquid peace that flowed within him and around him. For once, his mind was quiet and did not object with doubts or sharp remarks. It too was saturated with peace.

Benjamin was taken, still filthy and in his prison garb, back to his apartment and left there.

His flat-mates were thrilled, and utterly astonished that anyone could enter the Egyptian prison system and come out again. Their joy knew no bounds. They also told him proudly how they had fixed that traitor Husni Uthman. And Ben, even though he regretted their actions, let them revel in their loyalty to him. He recognized the friendship and affection that lay behind it.

Once he had taken a long hot bath, shaved, and dressed in his own clothes, he felt a bit more like himself. The other young men had induced the cook, Sitt Haseeba, to prepare a holiday feast for them, with roast lamb and chicken, and every other special food they could think of.

He waited a day to tell them that he was going to have to leave Egypt. They were not surprised. "*Ya Binyameen*," Abbas Bahri objected, sadly. "You have only just arrived. One year and a little more, that is nothing. Though it probably seems longer to you. There is so much more that you could have done here. Once again, you are leaving the *mulid* with no chickpeas."

"Wait, what does that mean, again?"

"You know, we say it of a man who missed his chance. He never got what he wanted."

"Oh, you can't say that of me, then," said Ben. "I made friends, I had work, I learned a lot, I escaped with my life." This made them laugh. *And I found love*, Ben thought, silently.

His next priority was to see Penelope Prior. He went to the Reed residence as soon as he decently could. The Reeds found a way to leave the two young people alone.

Benjamin held her close while she wept. They were tears of joy and relief, and deep tenderness. Suddenly losing him—perhaps forever—had concentrated Penny's mind wonderfully. She was now ready to commit herself in a way that might not have happened so quickly otherwise.

In those days, the rituals of courting were so standardized that it was clear what each small breakthrough signified and how it should come about. Permission to call, exchange of pleasantries, deeper communication, personal notes and letters, going out together, becoming known to one's family and friends. There were several stages to pass through, yet. Penny was still very young—only twenty-one years old—and Benjamin not much older. They had time. There were mothers to consult, siblings to inform, plans to make. But the essential fact was this: they were in love.

And they were not going to part, since both of them could now be employed on the staff of the Near East Relief in Syria. They must leave Egypt, but they had somewhere to go.

Benjamin had many practical arrangements to make within the allotted two-week interval. He concentrated on getting those things done. And then, he had the final challenge: saying farewell to his intimate friend, Mourad.

They met several times during those two weeks, but each of them knew which meeting was the last. They sat together, privately, in Doctor Mourad's apartment at the Tanta Hospital, where their relationship began.

Mourad had met Penny now and was caught up on that situation. They discussed their arrangements for travel; Ben's belongings had already been shipped.

They sat at the table in the corner of his apartment that served as a kitchenette. As they talked, Mourad kept his hands busy making coffee for them in a small brass vessel over his gas ring. He added the right amount of sugar to make it *mazbout*, because he knew that Ben preferred it that way. He did not trust his own emotions and tried to keep their conversation on a smooth and shallow level. But his friend wasn't prepared for that.

"I'll tell you, a few things are still bothering me," Ben began. "I keep comparing the way I was treated to the way those men at Danasur were treated. I mean, being in jail was not pleasant, but I got a fair hearing from the judges. And because the evidence was lacking, I was cleared and released. Suppose those men at Danasur had enjoyed the privileges of a foreign national. Suppose they had been represented by a lawyer from the American Consulate. I mean, Fauber actually *was* guilty, and even he was merely expelled from the country. It isn't right, and I'm having trouble with it."

"Egyptians do not expect justice from the government. We expect self-seeking, and favoritism, and caprice. And once in a while, an inexplicable bit of mercy, which of course is an act of God."

"Did God intervene for me? I know Mr. Bradley did."

"Benjamin, this is why the missionary here is regarded as a tool of the mighty and pitiless Western nations which stand in back of him with their mailed fists. With that much power, you don't need God."

Ben flinched as if Mourad had hit him.

After a moment he said, "Another thing that I can't stop thinking about. That boy Gamahl. I did my best to get through to him. But I got nowhere."

"Pffft! His mind is salt."

"What?"

"It's what the farmers say. Nothing grows in salt, or in salt water. You could not plant anything in Gamahl's mind . . . he was a field of salt."

"Oh, Mourad. Nobody is hopeless, surely. I just wish . . . actually, I was going to ask you to reach out to him. Try to find out if he is okay, and tell him I forgive him."

Mourad frowned. "I do not think I am able to do that."

"All right . . . never mind." Benjamin sighed. "I've been on the mission field for a year, and I never had an effect on anyone. I led no one to Christ. The S.V.M. society back at Yale would be extremely unimpressed."

"I must contradict you, there," Mourad said. "You can't conclude that. There may be . . . that is, you might have influenced persons without being aware of it."

"Perhaps. I think it's very unlikely, though."

"I consider it all but certain."

"I thought it was enough to try to love my neighbors, and even my enemies. I did try to do that. Have you read the Gospel of John?"

"No, I'm still in the Gospel of Matthew."

Ben looked at him, confused. "What do you mean, 'still'?"

"Nothing," said Mourad awkwardly. "I mean I read only Matthew, long ago you know, at Asyut College. In school."

"Okay . . . well . . . in John's Gospel, Jesus sums up his instructions to his followers: 'Love one another as I have loved you.' And he loved them by teaching them, healing them, leading them . . . and ultimately giving his life for them. Not by ruling over his people, but by serving them and suffering for them. That's our standard. It's a very tough one to meet."

"I suppose so."

"Well . . . listen, my dear friend . . . I need to get going soon, but first we have a bit of business to attend to." Benjamin reached into a bag he was carrying and pulled out a thick folder of papers. "I got Mr. Bradley's help with another couple of matters here. This is the first one."

He slid a packet of bank documents across the table to Mourad. "I asked him to research how much one would need to invest in order to open a specialist consultancy practice in Tanta. In pulmonary medicine. Experts told him that one could get started with about thirty thousand pounds. These papers show that we have deposited that much in an account in your name at the Bank Misr."

Mourad stared at the papers, uncomprehending.

"Also, we were able to buy the flat I was living in with the fellows on Muhammad Pasha Said Street," said Ben, producing another packet of papers and a property deed. "That's in your name, too. All I ask is that you allow them to go on living there while you get your practice started. They will soon finish their first posting and get reassigned by the Ministry of Education . . . I gather that their first appointment is usually two to three years. Then, you can fix up the flat and move in. Maybe there will be a Mrs. Mourad by that time."

The doctor's face was stunned.

"Now, this assumes that you will open your practice here in Tanta, and not move up to Cairo. There are lots of pulmonary specialists there, I think. But here in Tanta, they need you. Philip Hessburgh would be very disappointed in me if I caused you to flee to greener pastures. So I hope you will stay here. But the money and the apartment belong to you, so you can make that decision. You can take the money, sell the flat, and move on if you wish. No strings attached, as we say."

"Benjamin . . ." said Mourad, his voice hoarse.

"Please don't make a big issue of this, because it's already done. But if you need any legal advice, here is Mr. Bradley's contact information. I have retained him privately, as it were, to help you with any snags that might arise."

Mourad looked down, shaking his head.

"You are helping me, by accepting this," Ben said. "I need to feel that I have made some contribution to Egypt while I was here. I think this is the best I can do."

There was a bit more talk, and many blessings exchanged, and a last fond embrace. And then Benjamin left.

Mourad walked around for several days like a man in a trance. He saw patients, he made dinner, he carried on with daily life, but between manifestations of Jesus and the unexpected donation of Ben Channing, his mind was in a scramble. At last he went to see Philip Hessburgh to talk to him about moving to a consultancy instead of a residency practice and the impact it would have on Tanta Hospital. He discovered that Doctor

Hessburgh already knew all about it and heartily approved. Ben had taken care of this, too.

On that Friday morning, Mourad awoke early, even though it was his day off. And immediately he was flooded again with that sense of infinite peace. *Peace I leave with you, my peace I give unto you; not as the world giveth, give I unto you.*

He got up, got dressed, and walked over to al-Bahnasi Street, to the Egyptian Protestant church.

SELECTED SOURCES

Badrawi, Malak. *Political Violence in Egypt 1910–1924: Secret Societies, Plots, and Assassinations*. Surrey: Curzon, 2000.

Baedeker, Karl. *Egypt and the Sûdân: Handbook for Travellers*. Leipzig: Karl Baedeker, 1929.

Baron, Beth. *The Orphan Scandal: Christian Missionaries and the Rise of the Muslim Brotherhood*. Stanford: Stanford University Press, 2014.

Beatty, Sherrard. *Incidents in Rescue Mission Work*. Cincinnati: Rescue Mission, 1895.

Blackman, Winifred S. *The Fellahin of Upper Egypt: Their Religious, Social and Industrial Life with Special Reference to Survivals from Ancient Times*. London: George G. Harrap, 1927.

Blunt, Wilfrid Scawen. *Atrocities of Justice under British Rule in Egypt*. 2nd ed. London: T. Fisher Unwin, 1907.

———. *My Diaries: Being a Personal Narrative of Events 1888–1914*. Vol. 2, 1900–1914. New York: Alfred A. Knopf, 1921.

Boulos, Samir. *European Evangelicals in Egypt (1900–1956): Cultural Entanglements and Missionary Spaces*. Leiden: Brill, 2016.

Boyle, Stephanie Anne. "Sickness, Scoundrels and Saints: Tanta in the World and the World in Tanta, 1856–1907." Ph.D. dissertation, Northeastern University, 2012.

Brent, Chares H. *Adventure for God*. New York: Longmans, Green and Co., 1905.

Brinton, Jasper Yeates. *The Mixed Courts of Egypt*. New Haven: Yale University Press, 1930.

Brown, Arthur Judson. *The Foreign Missionary: Incarnation of a World Movement*. New York: Fleming H. Revell, 1907.

Brundage, John F. and G. Dennis Shanks. "Deaths from Bacterial Pneumonia during the 1918–19 Influenza Pandemic." *Emerging Infectious Diseases* 14/8 (Aug 2008) 1193–1199.

Burke, Jeffrey C. "The Establishment of the American Presbyterian Mission in Egypt, 1854–1940: An Overview." Ph.D. dissertation, McGill University, 2000.

Butcher, Edith Louise. *Things Seen in Egypt*. London: Seeley and Service, 1923.

The Call, Qualifications and Preparation of Candidates for Foreign Missionary Service. New York: Student Volunteer Movement for Foreign Missions, 1906.

Campbell, Charles S. *William Whiting Borden: A Short Life Complete in Christ*. New Haven: Yale, [1913].

Carter, Barbara L. "On Spreading the Gospel to Egyptians Sitting in Darkness: The Political Problem of Missionaries in Egypt in the 1930s." *Middle Eastern Studies* 20/4 (Oct 1984) 18–36.

Coles, Charles E. [Pasha]. *Recollections and Reflections*. London: Saint Catherine Press, 1918.

Colla, Elliott. *Conflicted Antiquities: Egyptology, Egyptomania, Egyptian Modernity*. Durham: Duke University Press, 2007.

Delta Evangelistic Committee. American Mission in Egypt. *Minutes*. Unpublished records, 1923–26.

Descriptive Guide to the Nile Mission Press Publications Suitable for Workers among Moslems, Jews and Christians. Cairo: Nile Mission Press, 1913.

Dewairy, Metry Saleeb. "The Contribution of the Western Church." In *Voices from the Near East*, ed. by Milton Stauffer, 79–100. New York: Student Volunteer Movement for Foreign Missions, 1927.

Ener, Mine. *Managing Egypt's Poor and the Politics of Benevolence, 1800–1952*. Princeton: Princeton University Press, 2003.

Erdman, Charles R. *An Ideal Missionary Volunteer: A Sketch of the Life and Character of William Whiting Borden*. Wimbledon: South Africa General Mission, [1913].

Finney, Davida. *Tomorrow's Egypt*. Pittsburgh: Women's General Missionary Society, 1939.

Goldberg, Ellis. "Peasants in Revolt—Egypt 1919." *International Journal of Middle East Studies* 24/2 (May 1992) 261–80.

Gollock, Minna C. *River, Sand, and Sun: Being Sketches of the C.M.S. Egypt Mission*. London: Church Missionary House, 1906.

Gorman, Anthony. "Regulation, Reform and Resistance in the Middle Eastern Prison." In *Cultures of Confinement: A History of the Prison in Africa, Asia and Latin America*, ed. by Frank Dikötter and Ian Brown, 95–146. Cornell University Press, 2007.

Hadley, Samuel H. *Down in Water Street*. New York: Fleming H. Revell, 1906.

Hafez, Nagwa Abdel-Wahab. "School Status and Delinquent Behavior among Youth in the Arab Republic of Egypt." Ph.D. dissertation, Florida State University, 1977.

Hogg, Rena. *Letters* [from a missionary journey on the Nile]. In manuscript, 1909.

Hoyle, Mark S.W. "The Mixed Courts of Egypt, 1916–1925." *Arab Law Quarterly* 2/3 (Aug 1987) 292–310. See also *Mixed Courts of Egypt*, London: Graham & Trotman, 1991.

Humphreys, Andrew. *Grand Hotels of Egypt in the Golden Age of Travel*. Cairo: American University in Cairo Press, 2011.

Hutchison, R. C. "Islam and Christianity." *Atlantic Monthly* 138 (Nov. 1926) 706–10.

Krämer, Gudrun. *Hasan al-Banna*. Oxford: Oneworld, 2010.

Lanfranchi, Sania Sharawi. *Casting Off the Veil: The Life of Huda Shaarawi, Egypt's First Feminist*. London: I. B. Tauris, 2012.

Lautz, Terrill E. "The S.V.M. and the Transformation of the Protestant Mission to China." In *China's Christian Colleges: Cross-Cultural Connections, 1900–1950*, ed. by Daniel H. Bays and Ellen Widmer, 1–22. Stanford: Stanford University Press, 2009.

Leeder, S. H. *Modern Sons of the Pharaohs: A Study of the Manners and Customs of the Copts of Egypt*. London: Hodder and Stoughton, [1918].

Lia, Brynjar. *The Society of the Muslim Brothers in Egypt: The Rise of an Islamic Mass Movement, 1928–1942*. Reading: Ithaca, 1998.

Luke, Kimberly. "Order or Justice: The Denshawi Incident and British Imperialism." *History Compass* 5/2 (2007) 278–87.

Mahfouz, Naguib. *Palace of Desire*. Trans. by W. M. Hutchins, Lorne and Olive Kenny. Cairo: American University in Cairo Press, 1991.

Mak, Lanver. *The British in Egypt: Community, Crime and Crises, 1822–1922*. London: I. B. Tauris, 2012.

Marshall, J. E. "The Egyptian Penal Code: Its Failure to Reduce Crime to a Normal Level." *L'Egypte Contemporaine* 13 (1922) 324–31.

———. "Prison Reform." *L'Egypte Contemporaine* 12 (1921) 476–86.

Mayeur-Jaouen, Catherine. *The Mulid of al-Sayyid al-Badawi of Tanta: Egypt's Legendary Sufi Festival.* Trans. by Colin Clement. Cairo: American University in Cairo Press, 2019.

Milner, Edward [Viscount]. *England in Egypt.* 13th ed. London: Edward Arnold, 1920.

Missionary Association. American Mission in Egypt. *Minutes.* Asyut, 27 January–5 February 1914.

Mitchell, Richard P. *The Society of the Muslim Brothers.* New York: Oxford University Press, 1993.

Naguib, Nefissa and Inger Marie Okkenhaug. *Interpreting Welfare and Relief in the Middle East.* Leiden: Brill, 2008.

Ordinary Lives and Grand Schemes: An Anthropology of Everyday Religion. Ed. by Samuli Schielke and Lisa Debevec. New York: Berghahn Books, 2012.

Owen, Roger. *Lord Cromer: Victorian Imperialist, Edwardian Proconsul.* Oxford: Oxford University Press, 2004.

Parker, Michael. *The Kingdom of Character: The Student Volunteer Movement for Foreign Missions (1886–1926).* Lanham: University Press of America, 1998.

Peters, Rudolph. "Controlled Suffering: Mortality and Living Conditions in 19th-Century Egyptian Prisons." *International Journal of Middle East Studies* 36/3 (Aug 2004) 387–407.

———. "Egypt and the Age of the Triumphant Prison: Legal Punishment in Nineteenth Century Egypt." *Annales Islamologiques* 36 (2002) 253–85.

Putney, Clifford. *Muscular Christianity: Manhood and Sports in Protestant America, 1880–1920.* Cambridge, MA: Harvard University Press, 2001.

Rees, Seth Cook. *Miracles in the Slums.* Chicago: S.B. Shaw, 1905.

Reeves, Edward. "Power, Resistance, and the Cult of Muslim Saints in a Northern Egyptian Town." *American Ethnologist* 22/2 (May 1995) 306–23.

Reeves, Nicholas and John H. Taylor. *Howard Carter Before Tutankhamun.* London: British Museum, 1992.

Rifat, Mansur Mustafi. *Damaging Evidence against English Hypocrisy.* Berlin: [s.n.], 1915.

Rindge, Fred H. "Human Engineering: How the Young Men's Christian Association is Reaching Industrial Workers." *The American City* 16/6 (June 1917) 584–86.

Ryad, Umar. "Muslim Response to Missionary Activities in Egypt: With a Special Reference to the Al-Azhar High Corps of 'Ulamâ (1925–1935)." In *New Faith in Ancient Lands: Western Missions in the Middle East in the Nineteenth and Early Twentieth Centuries,* ed. by Heleen Murre-van den Berg, 281–307. Leiden: Brill, 2006.

Sami, Ahmed. "Juvenile Vagrants and Delinquents." *L'Égypte Contemporaine* 14 (Mar 1923) 250–272.

Sattin, Anthony. *Lifting the Veil: British Society in Egypt, 1768–1956.* London: J. M. Dent, 1988.

Saunders, J. Roscoe. *Men and Methods That Win in the Foreign Fields.* New York: Fleming H. Revell, 1921.

Schielke, Samuli. "On Snacks and Saints: When Discourses of Rationality and Order Enter the Egyptian *mawlid.*" *Archives de Sciences Socials des Religions* 51/135 (Jul–Sep 2006) 117–40.

Sedra, Paul. *From Mission to Modernity: Evangelicals, Reformers, and Education in Nineteenth-Century Egypt.* New York: I. B. Tauris, 2011.

Shaarawi, Huda. *Harem Years: The Memoirs of an Egyptian Feminist, 1879–1924.* Trans. and ed. by Margot Badran. New York: City University of New York, 1987.

Sharkey, Heather J. *American Evangelicals in Egypt: Missionary Encounters in an Age of Empire.* Princeton : Princeton University Press, 2008.

———. "American Missionaries in Egypt, Gender Relations, and the Professional and Social Formation of Women." *Social Sciences and Missions* 34 (2021) 62–91.

———. "Arabic Antimissionary Treatises: Muslim Responses to Christian Evangelism in the Modern Middle East." *International Bulletin of Missionary Research* 28/3 (Jul 2004) 98–106.

———. "Empire and Muslim Conversion: Historical Reflections on Christian Missions in Egypt." *Islam and Christian-Muslim Relations* 16/1 (Jan 2005) 41–60.

Shelley, Michael T. "The Life and Thought of W. H. T. Gairdner, 1873–1928: A Critical Evaluation of a Scholar-Missionary to Islam." Ph.D. dissertation, University of Birmingham, 1988.

Showalter, Nathan D. *The End of a Crusade: The Student Volunteer Movement for Foreign Missions and the Great War.* Lanham, MD: Scarecrow, 1998.

Skreslet, Paula Youngman and Rebecca Skreslet. *The Literature of Islam: A Guide to the Primary Sources in English Translation.* Lanham, MD: Scarecrow, 2006.

Sladen, Douglas. *Egypt and the English.* London: Hurst & Blackett, 1908.

———. *Oriental Cairo: The City of the "Arabian Nights."* London: Hurst & Blackett, 1911.

Smith, Fred B. *A Man's Religion.* New York: Association Press, 1913.

———. "Will Christianity Win?" *Missionary Review of the World* 38/1 (Jan. 1915) 29–33.

Smith, Harry Lee. Letter to Samuel M. Zwemer, 15 January 1916. Samuel Marinus Zwemer personal papers, Presbyterian Historical Society.

Spooner, Lesley H. "The Specific Diagnosis and Treatment of Acute Lobar Pneumonia." *New England Journal of Medicine* 182/9 (26 Feb 1920) 224–28.

Stanley, Brian. *The Bible and the Flag: Protestant Missions and British Imperialism in the Nineteenth and Twentieth Centuries.* Leicester: Apollos, 1990.

Swan, George. *Lacked Ye Anything? A Brief Story of the Egypt General Mission.* Rev. ed. London: Egypt General Mission, 1932.

Taylor, Mary G. (Mrs. Howard Taylor). *Borden of Yale '09: "The Life That Counts."* Philadelphia: China Inland Mission, 1927.

Thackeray, Lance. *The People of Egypt.* London: Adam & Charles Black, 1910.

Thompson, Andrew A. "Village Schools in the Delta." *The United Presbyterian* 69/25 (22 June 1911) 18.

Thompson, Anna Y. "The Woman Question in Egypt." *Moslem World* 4/3 (July 1914) 266–72.

Tyndale, Walter. *Below the Cataracts.* London: William Heinemann, 1907.

United Presbyterian Church of North America. *Annual Report of the Board of Foreign Missions.* Philadelphia: U.P.C.N.A. 1915–1916.

United Presbyterian Church of North America. *Minutes of the General Assembly.* Pittsburgh: Board of Education of the U.P.C.N.A. Vol. 15, nos. 1–4, 1920–1923.

United Presbyterian Church of North America. *Triennial Report of the Board of Foreign Missions.* Philadelphia: U.P.C.N.A. 1919–1921, 1922–1924.

United Presbyterian Church in the U.S.A. Commission on Ecumenical Mission and Relations. Missionary and General Correspondence, 1860–1966. Subseries 1: Egypt. Box 6, Folder 35. Zwemer, Samuel Marinus, 1913–1919. At the Presbyterian Historical Society.

Wahba, Tharwat. *The Practice of Mission in Egypt: A Historical Study of the Integration Between the American Mission and the Evangelical Church in Egypt, 1854–1970.* Carlisle: Langham, 2016.

Washburn, B. E. "Use of Thymol in Treatment of Hookworm Disease." *Journal of the American Medical Association* 68/16 (21 April 1917) 1162–1163.

Wilbur, Susan Warren. *Egypt and the Suez Canal.* Burton Holmes Travel Stories series. Chicago: Wheeler, 1927.

Wood, Leonard. *Islamic Legal Revival: Reception of European Law and Transformations in Islamic Legal Thought in Egypt, 1875–1952.* Oxford: Oxford University Press, 2016.

Zalaf, Ahmed Abou El. "The Special Apparatus (al-Nizam al-Khass): The Rise of Nationalist Militancy in the Ranks of the Egyptian Muslim Brotherhood." *Religions* 13/1 (14 Jan 2022) item 77.

Zwemer, Samuel M. "Attitude of Moslems in Egypt Toward the Gospel." *The United Presbyterian* 76 (25 July 1918) 12–13.

———. *The Disintegration of Islam.* New York: Fleming H. Revell, 1916.

———. *Islam: A Challenge to Faith.* 2nd rev. ed. New York: Student Volunteer Movement for Foreign Missions, 1909.

———. *The Throne Verse.* Cairo: Nile Mission Press, undated.

———. *The Unoccupied Mission Fields of Africa and Asia.* New York: Student Volunteer Movement for Foreign Missions, 1911.

www.ingramcontent.com/pod-product-compliance
Lightning Source LLC
Chambersburg PA
CBHW071225260626
47162CB00004B/1422